“Why did he come c
asked. “I thought you shot him back at the camp.”

“Obviously it wasn’t enough to stop him.”

“But he won’t stop us.”

“No, he won’t.” He started out of the culvert, but she took hold of his arm, turning him toward her.

“What—” She cut off the question, her lips on his, her body pressed against him. All the fear and anxiety and the giddy relief of being alive at this moment coalesced in that kiss.

He wrapped his arms around her, crushing her to him. Every kiss touched some vulnerable part of her, coaxing her to let go a little bit more, to surrender. To trust.

He rested his forehead against hers. “This isn’t the best time for this,” he said.

“I know. We have to go. I just... I wanted you to know how I felt.”

“I got the message, loud and clear.” He wrapped both hands around her wrists and kissed the tips of her fingers, a gesture which set her heart to fluttering wildly.

UNDERCOVER HUSBAND

CINDI MYERS

Recycling programs for this product may not exist in your area.

ISBN-13: 978-1-335-72110-5

Undercover Husband

This is a work of fiction. Names, characters, places and incidents are either the product of the author's imagination or are used fictitiously, and any resemblance to actual persons, living or dead, business establishments, events or locales is entirely coincidental.

This edition published by arrangement with Harlequin Books S.A.

For questions and comments about the quality of this book, please contact us at CustomerService@Harlequin.com.

Printed in U.S.A.

Cindi Myers is the author of more than fifty novels. When she's not crafting new romance plots, she enjoys skiing, gardening, cooking, crafting and daydreaming. A lover of small-town life, she lives with her husband and two spoiled dogs in the Colorado mountains.

Books by Cindi Myers

Harlequin Intrigue

The Ranger Brigade: Family Secrets

Murder in Black Canyon
Undercover Husband

The Men of Search Team Seven

Colorado Crime Scene
Lawman on the Hunt
Christmas Kidnapping
PhD Protector

The Ranger Brigade

The Guardian
Lawman Protection
Colorado Bodyguard
Black Canyon Conspiracy

Rocky Mountain Revenge
Rocky Mountain Rescue

Visit the Author Profile page at Harlequin.com for more titles.

CAST OF CHARACTERS

Hannah Dietrich—A corporate chemist in Texas, Hannah is used to fighting her own battles and being in charge. But when her sister dies and names Hannah guardian of her infant daughter, Hannah will do anything to find and save the baby, even if it means temporarily surrendering control to someone else.

Walt Riley—The BLM Special Agent is an experienced investigator, but posing as Hannah's husband to infiltrate a back-to-nature cult tests him in ways he hasn't been tested before. Can he save Hannah and her niece without losing his heart in the process?

Daniel Metwater—Son of a wealthy industrialist, Metwater has forsaken his upbringing to preach peace and love to a wandering band of followers who are camping on public land. He calls himself a prophet, but the Ranger Brigade believes he's hiding a bigger secret, maybe even murder.

Emily Dietrich—The young woman left her home to join up with Metwater's "Family" after her fiancé was killed. Pregnant and alone, she put her trust in the Prophet, only to die alone in a Denver hospital under mysterious circumstances. She was one of Metwater's favorites, but did a falling out with him lead to her death?

Phoenix—The former heroin addict credits Metwater with saving her life. As one of his most loyal followers, she claims she would do anything for him, but does that include murder?

Kiram—Metwater's enforcer dislikes rule breakers and has a special hatred for Walt, who refuses to bend to his will.

Lucia Renfro—The teenager came to Metwater wanting to join the family. He says he sent her away, but now she's missing and all clues lead back to the camp.

Chapter One

"I was told you're the ones who can help me."

The soft, cultured voice as much as the words caught the attention of Bureau of Land Management special agent Walt Riley. The Ranger Brigade headquarters in Black Canyon of the Gunnison National Park didn't get many visitors, and certainly not many women as beautiful as the one standing on the opposite side of his desk now. Slender, with blond hair worn piled on top of her head, she spoke with an air of command, as if she was used to overseeing a corporation or running board meetings. Everything about her—from the designer sunglasses to the diamonds glinting at her earlobes to the toes of her high heels—looked expensive, and out of place in this part of rural Colorado, where jeans and boots were the most common attire for men and women alike.

Walt stood. "What do you need help with?" he asked. He selfishly hoped she wasn't merely a lost tourist or someone who needed a camping permit or something that was better handled by the park rangers in the office next door.

She opened the sleek leather satchel she had slung over one shoulder and pulled out a sheaf of papers and handed it to him. At first glance, it appeared to be some kind of legal document. "What is this?" he asked.

"It's a court order awarding me custody of my niece, Joy Dietrich." She removed the sunglasses and he found himself staring into a pair of intensely blue eyes, their beauty undimmed by the red rims and puffy lids, evidence that Miss Cool and Collected had, very recently, been crying. "I need your help getting her back from the people who have kidnapped her," she said.

This definitely was more serious than a camping permit. Walt dragged a chair over to his desk. "Why don't you sit down, Ms.—?"

"Dietrich. Hannah Dietrich." She sat, crossing her long legs neatly at the ankles. There was nothing particularly revealing about the gray slacks and matching jacket she wore, but she still managed to look sexy wearing them. Or maybe it was only that Walt had always had a thing for blue-eyed blondes.

"Wait here, Ms. Dietrich," he said. "I'm going to get my commanding officer and you can tell us your story."

He strode to the back of the building and poked his head around the open door of Commander Graham Ellison's office. The FBI agent, who still carried himself like the marine he had once been, broke off his conversation with DEA agent Marco Cruz. Elsewhere in the office or out in the field, officers from Immigration and Customs Enforcement, Customs and Border Protection, and Colorado State Patrol worked together to fight crime on thousands of acres of public land in the southwest corner of Colorado. Walt, one of the newest members of the Ranger team, had jumped at the opportunity to be involved in the kind of high-profile cases the Rangers were becoming known for. A kidnapping would definitely qualify as high-profile.

"Something up, Walt?" Graham asked.

"There's a woman out here who says she needs our help recovering her kidnapped niece," Walt said. "Before I had her run through the whole story, I thought you might like to hear it."

"Who does she say kidnapped her niece?" Marco, one of the senior members of the Ranger Brigade, had a reputation as an expert tracker and a cool head in even the tensest situations. Walt hadn't had a chance to work with him yet, but he had heard plenty of stories from others on the team.

"We haven't gotten that far yet," Walt said.

"Let's hear what she has to say." Graham led the way back to Walt's desk, where Hannah Dietrich waited. If the prospect of being confronted by three lawmen unsettled her, she didn't show it. "Ms. Dietrich, this is Commander Graham Ellison and Agent Marco Cruz."

"Hello." She nodded, polite but reserved. "I hope you'll be able to help me."

"Why don't you tell us more about your situation?" Graham pulled up a second chair, while Marco stood behind him. Walt perched on the corner of the desk. "You say your niece was kidnapped?"

"In a manner of speaking."

"What manner would that be?" Marco crossed his arms over his chest.

"I think it would be best if I began at the beginning." She smoothed her hands down her thighs and took a deep breath. "I have—had—a sister, Emily. She's six years younger than me, and though we have always been close, in temperament we're very different. She was always carefree, impulsive and restless."

Nothing about Hannah Dietrich looked restless or impulsive, Walt thought. Even obviously distressed as she was, the word she brought to mind was *control.* She controlled her feelings and she was used to being in control of her life.

"About a year ago, Emily met a man, Raynor Gilbert," Hannah continued. "He was working as a bouncer at a club in Denver that she used to frequent, and they became lovers. She found out she was pregnant, and they had plans to marry, but he was killed in a motorcycle accident only a week after Emily learned she was expecting." She paused a moment, clearly fighting for composure, then continued.

"My sister was devastated, and acted out her grief with even more impulsive behavior. I wanted her to come live with me, but she refused. She said she wanted a different life for herself and her child. She attended a rally by a group that calls themselves the Family. Their leader is a very handsome, charismatic man named Daniel Metwater."

"We know about Metwater." Graham's expression was grim. Metwater and his "family" had a permit to camp in the Curecanti National Recreation Area, adjacent to the national park and part of the Rangers' territory. Though Metwater had recently been eliminated as the chief suspect in a murder investigation, the Rangers continued to keep a close watch on him and his followers.

"Then you are probably aware that he recruits young people to join his group, promising them peace and harmony and living close to nature," Hannah said. "His message appealed to my sister, who I believe was looking for an excuse to run away from her life for a while."

"When was the baby—Joy—born?" Walt asked.

Her eyes met his, softening a little—because he had remembered the child's name? "She was born a little over three months ago. Emily sent me a letter with a photograph. She said the baby was healthy, but I know my sister well enough to read between the lines. I sensed she wasn't happy. She said things had been hard, though she didn't provide any details, and she said she wanted to come home for a visit but didn't know if the Prophet—that's what this Metwater person calls himself—would allow it. I would have gone to her right away, but her letter gave no clue as to where she was located. She said the Family was moving soon and she would write me again when they were settled."

"Did she usually contact you via letter instead of calling or texting or emailing?" Walt asked.

"Apparently, one condition of being a part of this group is giving up electronic devices like computers and cell phones," Hannah said. "I don't know if all the members comply with that restriction, but Hannah was very serious about it. Shortly after she joined the group, she wrote and told me we could only communicate through letters."

"Did that alarm you?" Graham asked.

"Of course it did." A hint of annoyance sharpened Hannah's voice. "I wrote back immediately and tried to persuade her that a group that wanted its members to cut off contact with family and friends had to be dangerous—but that letter came back marked Return to Sender. It was months before I heard anything else from Emily, and that was the letter informing me of Joy's birth. In the interim, I was worried sick."

She opened the satchel once more and withdrew an envelope. "Then, only two weeks after the letter announcing Joy's birth came, I received this." She handed the envelope to Walt. He pulled out two sheets of lined paper, the left edge ragged where the pages had been torn out of a notebook.

"'I'm very afraid. I don't think anyone can help me,'" Walt read out loud. "'If anything happens to me, promise you will take care of Joy.'" He looked at Hannah. "What did you do when you received this?"

"I was frantic to find her. I hired a private detective, and he was able to track down Metwater and his followers, but they told him there was no one in the group who fit my sister's description and they knew nothing. Look at the other paper, please."

Walt handed the first sheet to Graham and scanned the second sheet. "Is this a will?" he asked.

"Yes. It names me as Joy's guardian in the event of Emily's death. I was able to have a court certify it as legal and grant me custody."

"How did you do that?" Graham asked. "Without proof of your sister's death?"

"I was able to find proof." She brought out another envelope and handed it to the commander. "Here are copies of my sister's death certificate, as well as a birth certificate for her daughter."

Graham read the documents. "This says she died in Denver, of respiratory failure." He frowned. "Did your sister have a history of respiratory problems?"

"She had suffered from asthma off and on for most

of her life, but it was well controlled with medication. She never had to be hospitalized for it."

"Do you have any idea what she was afraid of?" Walt asked. "Did she specifically say that Metwater or anyone else threatened her?"

Hannah shook her head. "She didn't. But I know my sister. Emily was a lot of things, but she wasn't the nervous type and she wasn't a drama queen. She was truly terrified of something, and I think it had to do with Metwater and his cult."

Walt scanned the will again. His attention rested on the signatures at the bottom of the page. "This says the will was witnessed by Anna Ingels and Marsha Caldwell."

"Marsha Caldwell was a nurse at the hospital where Joy was born," Hannah said. "She left when her husband was transferred overseas, so I haven't been able to talk to her. And I wasn't able to determine who Anna Ingels is."

"Maybe she's one of Metwater's followers," Walt said.

"Except that most of them don't use their real names," Marco said. "It makes tracking them down more difficult."

"But not impossible," Graham said. He shuffled the papers in his hand. "This birth certificate says your niece was born in Denver. Have you talked with anyone there?"

"The hospital wouldn't give me any information,

and the PI wasn't able to find out anything, either." She shifted in her chair, as if impatient. "When I talked to the local sheriff's office, they said the area where Metwater is camping is your jurisdiction," she said. "All I need is for you to go with me to get Joy."

"You haven't tried to make contact with them on your own?" Graham asked.

She shook her head. "The private detective I hired paid them a visit. That's when they refused to admit they had ever known Emily or that Joy even existed. He told me the conditions in their camp are pretty rough—that it isn't the place for an infant." She pressed her lips together, clearly fighting to maintain her composure. "I don't want to waste any more time. I thought it would be better to show up with law enforcement backing. I know this Metwater preaches nonviolence, but my sister was genuinely afraid for her life. Why else would she have made a will at her age?"

"It doesn't seem out of line for a new parent to want to appoint a guardian for her child," Marco said. "Maybe she was merely being prudent."

"One thing my sister was not was prudent," Hannah said.

Unlike Hannah herself, Walt thought. He certainly knew how different siblings could be. "May I see the birth certificate?" he asked.

Graham passed it to him, then addressed Hannah. "Do you have a picture of your niece?"

"Only the newborn photo my sister sent." She slipped it from the satchel and handed it to him. Graham and Marco looked at it, then passed it to Walt.

He studied the infant's wrinkled red face in the oversize pink bonnet. "I don't think this is going to be much help in identifying a three-month-old," he said.

"We can go to Metwater and demand he hand over the child," Graham said. "But if he refuses to admit she even exists, it could be tougher."

"You can't hide an infant for very long," Hannah said. "Someone in the camp—some other mother, perhaps—knows she exists."

"What makes you think Metwater's group has her?" Marco asked. "It's possible she ended up with Child Welfare and Protection in Denver after your sister's death."

"I checked with them. They have no record of her. I'm sure she's still with Metwater and his group."

"Why are you so sure?" Walt asked.

Her expression grew pinched. "Take another look at her birth certificate."

Walt studied the certificate, frowning.

"What is it?" Marco asked.

Walt looked up from the paper, not at his fellow officers, but at Hannah. "This says the child's father is Daniel Metwater."

HANNAH HELD HERSELF very still, willing herself not to flinch at the awful words. "That's a lie," she said.

"Emily was pregnant long before she ever met Daniel Metwater, and I know she was in a relationship with Raynor Gilbert. I have pictures of them together, and I talked to people at the club where he worked." The conversations had been excruciating, having to relive her sister's happiness over the baby and being in love, and then the grief when her dream of a storybook future was destroyed by Raynor's death. "They all say he and Emily were together—that he was the father of her baby. A simple DNA test will prove that."

"Yet the court was willing to grant you custody of the child?" Graham asked.

"Temporary custody," she said. "Pending outcome of the DNA test. Believe me, Commander, Daniel Metwater is not Joy's father. Her father was Raynor Gilbert and he's dead."

"Let us do some investigating and see what we can find out," Graham said. "But even if we locate an infant of the appropriate sex and age in the camp, unless Metwater and his followers admit it's your sister's child, we won't be able to do anything. If some other woman is claiming to be the infant's mother, you may have to go back to court to request the DNA testing before we can seize the child."

She stood, so abruptly her chair slid back with a harsh protest, and her voice shook in spite of her willing it not to. "If you won't help me, I'll get the child on my own."

"How will you do that?" Walt asked.

"I'll pretend I want to join the group. Once I'm living with them, I can find Joy and I'll leave with her."

She braced herself for them to tell her she couldn't do that. Their expressions told her plainly enough that's what they were thinking—at least what the commander and Agent Cruz thought. Agent Riley looked a little less stern. "You've obviously given this some thought," he said.

"I will do anything to save my niece," she said. "I had hoped to do this with law enforcement backing, but if necessary, I will go into that camp and steal her back. And I dare you and anyone else to try to stop me."

Chapter Two

Daniel Metwater and his followers had definitely chosen a spot well off the beaten path for their encampment. After an hour's drive over washboard dirt roads, Walt followed Marco down a narrow footpath, across a plank bridge over a dry arroyo, to a homemade wooden archway that proclaimed Peace in crooked painted lettering. "Looks like they've made themselves at home," Walt observed.

"They picked a better spot this time." Marco glanced back at Walt. "You didn't see the first camp, did you?"

Walt shook his head. While several members of the team had visited Metwater's original camp as part of the murder investigation, he had been assigned to other duties.

"It was over in Dead Horse Canyon," Marco said. "No water, not many trees and near a fairly popular hiking trail." He looked around the heavily wooded spot alongside a shallow creek. "This is less exposed, with access to water and wood."

"Their permit is still only for two weeks," Walt said.

"There's plenty of room in the park for them to move around," Marco said. "And Metwater has some kind of influence with the people who issue the permits. They appear happy to keep handing them out to him."

A bearded young man, barefoot and dressed only in a pair of khaki shorts, approached. "Hello, Officers," he said, his expression wary. "Is something wrong?"

"We're here to see Mr. Metwater," Marco said.

"I'll see if the Prophet is free to speak with you," the man said.

"I think he understands by now it's in his best interest to speak with us," Marco said.

He didn't wait for the young man to answer, but pushed past him and continued down the trail.

The camp itself was spread out in a clearing some fifty yards from the creek—a motley collection of tents and trailers and homemade shelters scattered among the trees. A large motor home with an array of solar panels on the roof stood at one end of the collection. "That's Metwater's RV," Marco said, and led the way toward it.

Walt followed, taking the opportunity to study the men and women, and more than a few children, who emerged from the campers and tents and trailers to stare at the two lawmen. More than half the people he saw were young women, several with babies or toddlers in their arms or clinging to their skirts. The men he saw were young also, many with beards and longer hair, and all of them regarded him and Marco with expressions ranging from openly angry to guarded.

Marco rapped on the door to the large motor home. After a few seconds, the door eased open, and a strikingly beautiful, and obviously pregnant, blonde peered out at them. "Hello, Ms. Matheson." Marco touched the brim of his Stetson. "We'd like to speak to Mr. Metwater."

Frowning at the pair of officers, she opened the door wider. "I don't know why you people can't leave him alone," she said.

Walt had heard plenty about Andi Matheson, though he hadn't met her before. Her lover was the man murdered outside the Family's camp, and her father, a US senator, had been involved in the crime. She was perhaps the most famous of Metwater's followers, and apparently among those closest to him.

"We need to ask him some questions." Marco moved past her. Walt followed, nodding to Andi as he passed, but she had already looked away, toward the man who was entering from the back of the motor home.

Daniel Metwater had the kind of presence that focused the attention of everyone in the room on him. A useful quality for someone who called himself a prophet, Walt thought. Metwater was in his late twenties or early thirties, about five-ten or five-eleven, with shaggy dark hair and piercing dark eyes, and pale skin that showed a shadow of beard even in early afternoon. He wore loose linen trousers and a white cotton shirt unbuttoned to show defined abs and a muscular chest. He might have been a male model or a pop singer instead of an itinerant evangelist. "Officers." He nodded in greeting. "To what do I owe this pleasure?"

"We're looking for an infant," Marco said. "A little girl, about three months old."

"And what—you think this child wandered in here on her own?" Metwater smirked.

"Her mother was a follower of yours—Emily Dietrich," Marco said.

Metwater frowned, as if in thought, though Walt suspected the expression was more for show. "I don't recall a disciple of mine by that name," he said.

Walt turned to Andi. "Did you know Emily?" he asked.

She shook her head.

"What about Anna Ingels?" Walt asked.

Something flickered in her eyes, but she quickly looked away, at Metwater. "We don't have anyone here by that name, either," Metwater said.

"I asked Miss Matheson if she knows—or knew—of an Anna Ingels." Walt kept his gaze fixed on Andi.

"No," she said.

"Asteria, you may leave us now," Metwater said.

Andi—whose Family name was apparently Asteria—ducked her head and hurried out of the room. Metwater turned back to the Rangers. "What does any of this have to do with your missing infant?" he asked.

"Her aunt, Hannah Dietrich, came to us. She thinks her sister's child is here in this camp," Marco said. "She has legal custody of the baby and would like to assume that custody."

"If she believes this child is here, she's been misinformed," Metwater said.

"Then you won't mind if we look around," Walt said.

"We have a number of children here in the camp," Metwater said. "But none of them are the one you seek. I can't allow you to disrupt and upset my followers this way. If you want to search the camp, you'll have to get a warrant."

"This child's birth certificate lists you as the father," Marco said.

Metwater smiled, a cold look that didn't reach his eyes. "A woman can put anything she likes on a birth certificate," he said. "That doesn't make it true."

"Are you the father of any of the children in the camp?" Walt asked.

"I am father to all my followers," Metwater said.

"Is that how your followers—all these young women—see you?" Marco asked.

"My relationship to my disciples is a spiritual one," Metwater said. He half turned away. "You must excuse me now. I hope you find this child, wherever she is."

Walt's eyes met Marco's. The DEA agent jerked his head toward the door. "What do you think the odds are that his relationship with all these women is merely spiritual?" Walt asked once they were outside.

"About the same as the odds no one in this camp has a record or something they'd like to hide," Marco said.

"It does seem like the kind of group that would attract people who are running away from something," Walt said.

"Yeah. And everything Metwater says sounds like a lie to me," Marco said. He turned to leave, but Walt put out a hand to stop him.

"Let's talk to those women over there." He nodded toward a group of women who stood outside a grouping of tents across the compound. One of them stirred a pot over an open fire, while several others tended small children.

"Good idea," Marco said.

The women watched the Rangers' approach with wary expressions. Walt zeroed in on an auburn-haired woman who cradled an infant. "Hi," he said. "What's your baby's name?"

"Adore." She stroked a wisp of hair back from the baby's forehead.

"I think my niece is about that age," Walt said. "How old is she? About three months, right?"

"*He* is five months old," the woman said frostily, and turned away.

The other women silently gathered the children and went inside the tent, leaving Marco and Walt alone. "I guess she schooled you," Marco said.

"Hey, it was worth a try." He glanced around the camp, which was now empty. "What do we do now?"

"Let's get out of here." Marco led the way down the path back toward the parking area. They met no one on the trail, and the woods around them were eerily silent, with no birdsong or chattering of squirrels, or even wind stirring the branches of trees.

"Do you get the feeling we're being watched?" Walt asked.

"I'm sure we are," Marco said. "Metwater almost always has a guard or two watching the entrance to the camp."

"For a supposedly peaceful, innocent bunch, they sure are paranoid," Walt said. What did they have to fear in this remote location, and what did they have to protect?

Their FJ Cruiser with the Ranger Brigade emblem sat alone in the parking lot. Before they had taken more than a few steps toward it, Walt froze. "What's that on the windshield?" he asked.

"It looks like a note." Marco pulled out his phone and snapped a few pictures, then they approached slowly, making a wide circle of the vehicle first.

Walt examined the ground for footprints, but the

hard, dry soil showed no impressions. Marco took a few more close-up shots, and plucked the paper—which looked like a sheet torn from a spiral notebook—carefully by the edges. He read it, then showed it to Walt. The handwriting was an almost childish scrawl, the letters rounded and uneven, a mix of printing and cursive. "'All the children here are well cared for and loved,'" he read. "'No one needs to worry. Don't cause us any trouble. You don't know what you're doing.'"

He looked at Marco. "What do you think?"

"I'm wondering if the same person who left the note also left that." He gestured toward the driver's door of the cruiser, from which hung a pink baby bonnet, ribbons hanging loose in the still air.

"I'M SURE THIS is the same bonnet that's in the picture Emily sent me." Hannah fingered the delicate pink ribbons, the tears she was fighting to hold back making her throat ache. "Whoever left this must have wanted to let us know that Joy is there and that she's all right." She looked into Walt Riley's eyes, silently pleading for confirmation. The idea that anything might have happened to her niece was unbearable.

"We don't know why the bonnet was left," he said, his voice and his expression gentle. "But I agree that it looks very like the one in the picture you supplied us."

"What will you do now?" She looked at the trio of concerned faces. Agent Cruz and their commander had once again joined Walt to interview her at Ranger headquarters. She had broken the speed limit on the drive from her hotel when Walt had called and asked her to stop by whenever it was convenient.

"We're attempting to obtain a warrant to search the camp for your niece," the commander said. "We've also contacted Child Welfare and Protection to see if they've had any calls about the camp and might know anything."

That was it? When she had come to the Ranger office for help, she had expected them to immediately go with her to the Family's camp and take the child. When they had insisted on visiting the camp alone, she had held on to the hope that they would return with Joy. But they had done nothing but talk and ask questions. They seemed more interested in paperwork than in making sure Joy was safely where she belonged. "What am I supposed to do in the meantime?" she asked. "Just sit and wait?" And worry.

"I'm sorry to say that's all you can do right now," Agent Riley said. "Rushing in there on your own won't do anything but put Metwater and his people on the defensive. They might even leave the area."

"Then you could stop them," she said.

"On what grounds?" the commander asked. "So far we have no proof they've committed any crime."

"They have a child who doesn't belong to them, who isn't related to them in any way. A helpless infant." A child who was all she had left of her beloved sister.

"If they do have your niece, we don't have any reason to think they've harmed her or intend to harm her." Agent Riley reclaimed her attention with his calm voice and concerned expression. "The children we've seen in camp look well cared for, though we'll verify that with CWP."

"You're right." She clenched her hands in her lap and forced herself to take a deep breath. "Patience isn't one of my strong suits." Especially when it came to a baby. So much could go wrong, and could anyone who wasn't family watch over her as carefully as Hannah would?

"Go back to your hotel now," the commander said. "We'll be in touch." He and Agent Cruz left, leaving her alone with Agent Riley.

"I'll walk you to your car," he said.

"You didn't have to walk with me," she said, after they had crossed the gravel lot to the compact car she had rented at the Montrose airport. A brisk wind sent dry leaves skittering over the gravel and tugged strands of hair from her updo. She brushed the hair from her eyes and studied him, trying to read the expression behind his dark sunglasses.

"I wanted to talk to you a little more. Away from the office." He glanced back toward the low beige building that was Ranger headquarters. "Having to talk to a bunch of cops makes some people nervous."

"As opposed to talking to only one cop."

"Try to think of me as a guy who's trying to help."

"All right." She crossed her arms over her stomach. "What do you want to know?"

"I'm trying to figure out what Daniel Metwater stands to gain by claiming your niece is his daughter," he said. "Understanding people's motives is often helpful in untangling a crime."

"I imagine you know more about the man than I do. He's been living in this area for what, almost a month now?"

"About that. Is it possible your sister listed him as Joy's father without his knowledge?"

"Why would she do that?"

"You said she was one of his followers. He refers to himself as a father to his disciples. Maybe she was trying to honor that."

She studied the ground at her feet, the rough aggregate of rocks and dirt in half a dozen shades of red and brown. She might have been standing on Mars, for all she felt so out of her depth. "I don't know what my sister was thinking. As much as I loved her, I didn't understand her. She lived a very different life."

"Where do you live? I haven't even asked."

"Dallas. I'm a chemist." The expression on his face almost made her laugh. "Never play poker, Agent Riley."

"All right, I'll admit I'm surprised," he said. "I've

never met a female chemist before. Come to think of it, I may never have met a chemist before."

His grin, so boyish and almost bashful, made her heart skip a beat. She put her hand to her chest, as if to calm the irregular rhythm. "My job doesn't put me in contact with very many law enforcement officers, either." Impulsively, she reached out and touched his arm. "You'll let me know the minute you know anything about Joy? Call me anytime—even if it's the middle of the night."

He covered her hand with his own. The warmth and weight of that touch seeped into her, steadying her even as it made her feel a little off balance. "I will," he said. "And try not to worry. It may not seem like it, but we are doing everything we can to help you."

"I want to believe that." She pulled her hand away, pretending to fuss with the clasp of her handbag. "I'm used to being in charge, so it's not always easy to let someone else take over."

"Let us know if you think of anything that might be helpful."

"I will." They said goodbye and she got into her car and drove away. For the first time since coming to Colorado, she wasn't obsessing over Joy and Emily and the agonizing uncertainty of her situation. Instead, she was remembering the way it felt when Agent Walt Riley put his hand on hers. They had connected, something that didn't happen too often for her.

She had come into this situation thinking she was the only one who could save her niece. Maybe she wasn't quite so alone after all.

WALT SPENT EVERY spare moment over the next twenty-four hours working on Hannah's case. Though he prided himself on being a hard worker, the memory of Hannah's stricken face when he had last seen her drove him on. The afternoon of the second day, the Ranger team met to report on their various activities. Everyone was present except Montrose County sheriff's deputy Lance Carpenter, who was on his honeymoon but expected back later in the week, and Customs and Border Protection agent Michael Dance, who was following up a lead in Denver. After listening to a presentation by veteran Ranger Randall Knightbridge on a joint effort with Colorado Parks and Wildlife to catch poachers operating in the park, and a report from Colorado Bureau of Investigation officer Carmen Redhorse on an unattended death in the park that was ruled a suicide, Walt stood to address his fellow team members.

After a brief recap of Hannah's visit and his and Marco's foray into Metwater's camp, he consulted his notes. "I've gone over the documents Ms. Dietrich supplied us. We couldn't lift any useful prints from the letter or the will. Nothing on the note that was left at the camp, or the bonnet, either. I contacted the Denver hospital where the baby was born—the hat isn't one of theirs. They think the mother probably brought it with her, and they can't give out any information on patients. We're trying to reach the nurse who was one of the witnesses on Emily Dietrich's will, Marsha Caldwell. She is reportedly living in Amsterdam now, where her husband recently transferred for work, but I haven't gotten a response yet. We haven't had any luck locating the other witness, Anna Ingels."

"I talked to a contact at Child Welfare and Protection and she had nothing for me," Carmen said. "They did send a social worker to visit the camp a couple of weeks after Metwater and his group arrived here, but they found no violations. They said all the children appeared to be well cared for."

"And I don't guess they noted any baby crawling around with no mother to claim her," Ethan Reynolds, another of the new recruits to the Ranger Brigade, quipped.

"We got word a few minutes ago that the judge is denying our request for a warrant to search the camp," Graham said.

The news rocked Walt back on his heels, as if he'd been punched. "What was their reasoning?" he asked.

"We didn't present enough evidence to justify the search," the captain said. "At least in their eyes. The judge feels—and this isn't the first time I've heard this—that the Ranger Brigade's continued focus on Metwater and his followers is tantamount to harassment."

"This doesn't come from us," Randall said. "Ms. Dietrich came to us. She's the one who made the accusations against Metwater. We weren't harassing him. We were following up on her claim."

"And we found nothing," Graham said. He looked across the table and met Walt's steady gaze. "As long as Metwater and his people deny the baby exists, our hands are tied. There's nothing else we can do."

Chapter Three

Protests rose from all sides of the conference table after Graham's pronouncement. "We need to go back to the judge and try again," Michael Dance said.

"I can talk to Child Welfare and Protection," Carmen said. "Ask them to take another look."

"Unless we have CWP on our side, we're not going to get anywhere with this," Randall Knightbridge said.

Walt raised his voice to be heard over the clamor. "There's still something we can do, even without a warrant," he said.

Conversation died and everyone turned to look at him. "What do you have in mind?" Marco asked.

"I think we should do what Hannah suggested and infiltrate the group." Walt said.

"You mean, send someone in undercover to determine if the baby is really there?" Carmen asked.

"And maybe find out what really happened to the child's mother," Walt said. "Hannah said her sister was afraid for her life—maybe there's more to this story that we need to find out."

"It's not a bad idea," Graham said. "I've thought of it before, if only to get a better sense of what Metwater is up to."

"It could backfire, big time," said Simon Woolridge, tech expert and Immigration and Customs Enforcement agent. "If Metwater figures out what we're doing, he could take it to the press and gain a lot of traction with his claims that we're harassing him."

"He won't find out," Walt said. "Not if we do it right."

"By 'we' you mean who?" Graham asked.

Walt squared his shoulders. "I could go," he said. "I've done undercover work before."

"They'd recognize you," Marco said. "We were just at the camp this morning."

"I'd dye my hair and grown out my beard, and dress differently. They wouldn't recognize me as the lawman they saw one time."

"How are you going to know you found the right baby?" Carmen asked.

"Hannah Dietrich could come with me. I could say she's my sister."

"That won't work," Simon said. "You two don't look anything alike."

"Say she's your wife," Randall said. "From what we've seen, couples sometimes join Metwater's Family together."

"I could do that," Walt said. "If she agrees."

"You heard her," Marco said. "She'll do anything to save her niece."

"Talk to her," Graham said. "See what she says. But she has to agree to follow your lead and proceed with caution. And if you get in there and learn there's a real danger, you get out. No heroics."

"Yes, sir." He didn't want to be a hero. He only wanted to make things right for Hannah and her niece.

HANNAH HAD LOST the plot thread of the movie playing on the television in her hotel room an hour ago, but she left it on, grateful at least for the background noise that helped to make the room a little less forlorn. She glanced toward the porta-crib and the diaper bag in the corner of the room and felt a tight knot in her chest. Had she been naive to believe she would be bringing Joy back here last night, before heading back home to Dallas today? Now she was trapped in this awful limbo, not knowing when—or even if—she would see her niece.

A knock on the door startled her. She punched the remote to shut off the TV and moved to the door. A glimpse through the peephole showed Walt Riley, dressed not in his khaki uniform, but in jeans and a white Western-cut shirt. With trembling hands, she unfastened the security chain and opened the door. "Has something happened?" she asked. "Do you have news?"

"Hello, Ms. Dietrich," he said. "Can I come in? There are some things we need to talk about."

"All right." She stepped back and let him walk past her into the room. She caught the scent of him as he passed—not cologne, but a mixture of starch and leather that seemed imminently masculine.

He crossed the small room and sat in the only chair. She perched on the edge of the bed, her stomach doing nervous somersaults. "Were you able to get the warrant to search the camp?" she asked.

"No." He rested his hands on his knees. Large hands, bronzed from working in the sun, with short nails and no jewelry. "The judge didn't feel we had sufficient grounds to warrant a search. Metwater has complained we're harassing him, and the court is taking that complaint seriously."

"What about Child Welfare and Protection? Would they support you? Or go to the camp to look for Joy?"

He shook his head. "CWP says there aren't any problems at the camp. They would have no reason to be there."

She felt as if she had swallowed an anvil. The weight of it pressed her down on the bed. "What am I going to do now?" she asked.

"We've come up with a plan."

She leaned toward him. "What is it?"

"It's your plan, really. We'll send two people in, posing as a husband and wife who are interested in joining the Family. That will give us the opportunity to determine, first, if there is even an infant matching the description of your niece in the camp, and if her mother is there or not. We also hope to determine the circumstances surrounding your sister's death."

"I want to go. I want to be the woman."

"We're not talking a quick overnight visit," he said. "It could take weeks to gain their trust and learn anything of real value."

"I've taken a leave of absence from my job. I have however much time it takes."

"You said you're a chemist? Is your employer willing to let you off work indefinitely?"

"I'm very good at my job and I've been there a long time. I have savings and not many expenses. And when Joy comes to live with me, I intend to take family leave to spend time with her." She hoped that would give her enough time to adjust to being a mother—something she had never planned on being, but now wanted more desperately than she had wanted almost anything. "I want to do this, Agent Riley. I want to help find my niece."

"If you do this, you have to agree to follow the direction of the male agent who would be posing as your husband," he said. "You can't take any action without his knowledge and you have to agree to abide by his decisions."

She stiffened. "I'm not used to other people making decisions for me."

"Obviously not. But in this case it would be vital.

As law enforcement officers, we're trained to put together a case against someone that will stand up in court. If Daniel Metwater and his followers have kidnapped your niece, or if they had anything to do with your sister's death, we want to be sure we can build a solid case against them that will lead to a conviction."

What he said made sense, and she had always been good at following rules, as long as she saw a good reason for them. "All right. I can respect that," she said. "Who is the male agent?"

"That would be me."

She sat back a little, letting the words sink in. Relief that she wouldn't have to work with a stranger warred with the definite attraction that shimmered between them. She didn't need to be distracted right now. She had to focus on Joy, and the future they were going to have together. But what choice did she have? If she refused to work with Walt Riley just because she could imagine sleeping with him, wasn't she being foolish, and maybe even a coward? They were two adults. Surely they could control themselves. In any case, he had given no indication that he felt the same attraction to her. "All right," she said. "What do we do next?"

"Why don't we start by going out to dinner?"

Yet again, this man had caught her off guard. "Are you asking me on a date?"

"If we're going to pass ourselves off as husband

and wife, we need to know more about each other and get comfortable in each other's presence."

He was right, of course. "All right."

He stood and held out his hand. When she took it, he pulled her up beside him. "Why don't you start by calling me Walt?"

"All right. Walt." It wasn't so hard here, in the intimacy of her hotel room, to think of him by his first name. A simple and strong name, like the man himself. "You should call me Hannah."

"It's a nice name."

"I think so. I don't understand why so many of Metwater's followers feel compelled to take new names."

"It could be the symbolism of starting over, taking on a new identity," he said. "It's also a convenient way to make yourself harder to track down if you're wanted for a crime, or have something else in your past that you don't want to come out." He held the door as she walked through, then followed her outside. "Did your sister take a new name when she joined the group?"

"I don't know. She never mentioned it." She glanced over her shoulder at him. "I feel terrible that I don't know more about what my sister was doing in the last months of her life. A year ago, I would have said I knew her well, but so many times now, she feels like a stranger to me. It's depressing. You'd think if you could know anyone well, it would be a sibling."

"I think we're most surprised when family members behave in unexpected ways," he said. "It feels more personal, I guess. More like a betrayal."

"Yes." He opened the passenger-side door to his Cruiser and she climbed inside. He put a hand on her shoulder, as if making sure she was safely settled before he shut the door behind her. Again, she felt that current of connection with him. She hadn't felt anything like that—or rather, she hadn't allowed herself to feel it—for a very long time. Maybe losing Emily had made her more vulnerable. Or finding Joy. So many things in her life felt out of control these days, it shouldn't have surprised her that her emotions would betray her, too.

THERE WERE DEFINITELY worse ways to spend an evening than sitting across the table from a beautiful woman, Walt thought, once he and Hannah had settled into a booth at a local Italian place. More than one male head had turned to watch Hannah walk across the room, though maybe only Walt saw the fatigue and worry that lurked in her sapphire-blue eyes. He wished he had the power to take that worry and fatigue away from her.

"Tell me about yourself," he said, once they had placed their orders. "How long have you lived in Dallas?"

"Ten years. I took the job there after I got my master's at Rice University in Houston."

"So you're beautiful and brilliant. I'm already out of my league."

She sipped her iced tea and regarded him over the rim of the glass. "I don't know about that."

"Trust me, it's true," he said. "I have a bachelor's degree from the University of New Mexico and was solidly in the middle of my class. And while I'm sure there are a few professions less glamorous than law enforcement, patrolling the backcountry of public lands is about as far away from a corporate suite as you can get."

"Your job doesn't sound boring, though."

"You might be surprised how boring it can be sometimes. But mostly, it is interesting."

"What drew you to the work?" She relaxed back against the padded booth, some of the tension easing from around her eyes.

"I like the independence, and I like solving puzzles. And maybe this sounds corny, but I like correcting at least some of the injustice in the world. It's a good feeling when you put away a smuggler or a poacher or a murderer." His eyes met hers. "Or a kidnapper."

She rearranged her silverware. "Do you think this will work? Our pretending to want to join up with them?"

"It's the best way I can think of to learn what really goes on in their camp. I figure you can get to know the women—especially the mothers with children. I can talk to the men. We might be able to find Anna Ingels—the woman who witnessed your sister's will. If your niece is there, someone will know it and eventually they'll let something slip."

The waiter delivered their food—ravioli for Walt, fish for her. They ate in silence for a moment, then she said, "Have you done anything like this before?"

"You mean undercover work?" He stabbed at a pillow of ravioli. "A couple of times. I posed as a big-game hunter to bring down a group of poachers. And I did a few drug buys, things like that."

"Did you ever have to pretend to be married to someone?"

"No. That's a new one. Does that worry you?"

"A little. Not you, I mean—well, I've never been married before."

"Me either." He laid down his fork and wiped his mouth with his napkin. "Before we get too far into this, are you engaged? Seriously involved with someone? Dating a mixed martial arts fighter who's insanely jealous?"

Her eyes widened. "No to all of the above. What about you?"

"I don't have a boyfriend either. Or a girlfriend."

She laughed. "Really? That surprises me."

"Does it?"

"You're good-looking, and friendly. I wouldn't think you'd have trouble getting a date."

"No, I don't have trouble getting dates." He took

another bite of ravioli, delaying his answer. "I'm new to the area," he said. "I transferred from northern Colorado just last month."

"And?"

"And what?"

"And there's something you're not saying. I heard it in your voice."

Was he really so easy to read? He searched for some glib lie, but then again, why shouldn't he tell her? "The last woman I dated seriously is now married to my younger brother."

"Ouch!"

"Yeah, well, he's very charming and untroubled by much of a conscience." The wound still ached a little—not the woman's betrayal so much as his brother's. He should have seen it coming, and the fact that he hadn't made him doubt himself a little.

"So that's what you meant when you said you understood about thinking you knew a family member well, and turning out to be wrong."

"Yep. Been there, done that, got the T-shirt."

"That must make for some awkward family dinners," she said.

"A little. There are four of us kids—two girls and two boys. For the sake of family harmony, I wished the newlyweds well and keep my distance."

"It was just Emily and me in my family," she said. "I think it took my mom a long time to get pregnant again after me." A smile ghosted across her lips. "I still remember how excited I was when she was born. It was as if I had a real live doll of my own to look after. After our parents were killed in a car crash when Emily was nineteen, all we had was each other. We were inseparable, right up until I went away to Dallas to work. And even after that—even though we lived very different lives—I always felt we were close." She laid down her fork and her eyes met his. "I blamed Daniel Metwater for taking her away from me. After she joined his cult, I seldom heard from her. What kind of person encourages someone to cut off ties with family that way?"

"We haven't been able to learn a great deal about him, other than that he's very charismatic and seems to be offering something that some people find attractive." He wanted to take her hand, to try to comfort her, but resisted the temptation. "There are probably experts in this kind of thing who could tell you more than I can."

"He calls his followers a family—as if that could substitute for their real families."

"Maybe this undercover assignment will give you some of the answers to your questions," he said. He picked up his fork again.

They ate in silence for a while longer, until she pushed her plate away, her dinner half-eaten. "I've been thinking about what you asked me," she said. "About what Daniel Metwater stood to gain from keeping Joy and claiming her as his own."

"Did you come up with something?"

"It's not much, but Emily had a trust from our mother. An annual stipend now, with the bulk coming to her when she turned thirty in two years. Under the terms of the trust, it automatically passes to any children she might have, and can be used to pay living and educational expenses in the event of her death."

He considered this information, then shook his head. "Metwater supposedly has money of his own."

"That's what I understood from the research I did." She took a sip of tea. "I told you it wasn't much."

"Still, having money doesn't mean he might not want more. And we don't have any idea what his financial picture is these days. Maybe he made some bad investments, or being a prophet in the wilderness is more expensive than he thought it would be."

"I keep coming back to her last letter," Hannah said. "Emily sounded so frightened—I thought maybe that so-called Family was holding her prisoner."

"The death certificate said her cause of death was respiratory failure."

"I know. She died in an emergency room. Someone dropped her off—they don't know who. And people do die of asthma, but I can't help thinking—what if they were withholding her medication, or the stress of traveling with this group brought on the attack?"

"It would be tough to prove murder in either case."

"I know." She sat back and laid her napkin beside her plate. "And none of it will bring Emily back. I have to focus on what I can do, which is to raise Joy and take the best care of her I know how."

A light came into her eyes when she spoke, and her expression changed to one of such tenderness it made Walt's chest ache. "You already love her, don't you?" he said.

"Yes." That fleeting smile again. "And that surprises me. I never thought of myself as particularly nurturing, but this baby—this infant I haven't even met yet—I already love her so much."

"If she's in Metwater's camp, we'll find her," he said.

She surprised him by reaching out and taking his hand. "I believe you," she said. "And if I have to pretend to be someone's wife temporarily, I'm glad it's you."

He gave her hand a squeeze, then let it go before he gave in to the temptation to pull her close and kiss her. As assignments went, this one was definitely going to be interesting, and a little dangerous—in more ways than one.

Chapter Four

Two days later, Hannah studied herself in the hotel mirror, frowning. She wished she had taken more of an interest in drama club in school—she might have learned something that would come in handy now. The only advice Walt had given her was "Stick as close to the truth as possible and only lie when absolutely necessary." So she was going into camp as Hannah Morgan—her mother's maiden name—and she was a corporate dropout looking for a more authentic life.

She had dressed as Walt had instructed her, in a gauzy summer skirt, tank top and sturdy sandals. She wore no makeup and had combed out her hair to hang straight past her shoulders. Silver bracelets and earrings completed the look—definitely not her normal style, which tended toward plain classics, but that was all part of playing a role, wasn't it…dressing the part?

A knock on the door interrupted her musing. She checked the peephole, but didn't recognize the rumpled-looking man who stood on the other side.

Then he shifted so that the sun lit his face, and she sucked in a breath and jerked open the door. "I didn't recognize you at first," she said, staring at Walt. Several days' growth of beard darkened his jaw, giving him a rough—and definitely sexy—look. His hair was streaked blond and tousled and he wore jeans with a rip in one knee, hiking boots and a tight olive-green T-shirt that showed off a sculpted chest and defined biceps. A tribal tattoo encircled his upper right arm. Looking at him made her feel a little breathless.

"What do you think?" He held his arms out at his sides. "Will they still make me as a cop?"

Slowly, she shook her head. "No, I don't think so." *A biker or a bandit or an all-around bad boy, maybe, but not a cop.*

"You look great," he said. "I didn't realize your hair was so long."

She tucked a stray strand behind her ears. "I usually wear it up. It gets in the way otherwise."

"Are you ready to go? Marco just radioed that our contact is at the laundry."

She smoothed her sweating palms down her thighs and took a deep breath. "Yeah, I'm ready."

She collected the backpack into which she had stashed a few essentials and followed him across the parking lot. But instead of a car or truck, he stopped beside a motorcycle. The black-and-chrome monster looked large and dangerous. "We're going on that?" she asked.

He patted the leather seat. "I figured the Harley fit the image better. I've got a small tent and some other supplies in the saddlebags and trunk." He handed her a helmet. "Put this on."

She settled the helmet over her head. It was a lot heavier than she had expected. "Does this belong to the Rangers?" she asked, fumbling with the chin strap.

"No, it's my personal bike." He fastened the strap for her, a tremor running through her as his fingertips brushed across her throat. But he gave no sign that he noticed. He straddled the bike, then looked over his shoulder at her. "Get on behind me. Put your feet on the foot pegs."

Feeling awkward, she did as he instructed. "I've never ridden a motorcycle before," she said.

"Don't worry. Just hang on." She started as the engine roared to life, the sound vibrating through her. The bike lurched forward and she wrapped her arms around him, her breasts pressed against the solid muscle of his back, his body shielding hers from the wind. She forced herself to relax her death grip on him, but didn't let go altogether. He felt like the only steady thing in her world right now.

She tried to focus on the task ahead. Apparently, several women from Metwater's group came into town once a week to do laundry. The plan was for Walt and Hannah to meet them and turn the talk to the Family. They would express a desire to join the group and ask for an introduction. Walt had explained that interviews with some former group members had revealed this was how new members were often acquired. And Metwater had bragged on his blog that he didn't have to recruit members—they came to him voluntarily after hearing his message.

The laundry occupied the end unit of a low-slung building in a strip center not far from the campus of the local college. Though Metwater's three followers were the same age as many of the students who lounged on chairs between the washers and dryers or gathered in the parking lot, they looked somehow different. Their bare faces were pink from exposure to the sun, and their long skirts and sleeveless tops were faded and worn. One of the women had a baby on her hip, and Hannah couldn't keep from staring at the child, who wore a stained blue sleeper and had a shock of wheat-colored hair and plump, rosy cheeks.

"That's a beautiful baby," she said, forgetting that they had agreed she would let Walt do most of the talking.

"Thanks." The woman, who wore her light brown hair in two long braids, hefted the child to her shoulder, her eyes wary.

"How old is he?" Hannah asked. "Or she?"

"He's almost seven months," she said.

Hannah realized she had been staring at the child too intently. She forced a smile to her face. "I'm Hannah," she said. "And this is my husband, Walt. A friend told me she had seen you all doing your laundry here sometimes, so we came here hoping to meet some members of the Family."

"We've been reading the Prophet's blog," Walt said. "His message really spoke to us. We were wondering how we could go about joining the group."

The baby's mother looked over her shoulder, toward where the other two women were filling a row of washers. "You should talk to Starfall," she said. "Starfall! Come talk to these people."

Starfall had curly brown hair and a slightly crooked nose, and the beginnings of lines along each side of her mouth, as if she frowned a lot. She was frowning now as she approached them. "What do you want?" she asked.

"We wanted to know how we could go about joining up with the Family," Walt said. He took Hannah's hand and squeezed it. "We've been reading the Prophet's writing and we really like what he has to say."

"Is that so?" Starfall addressed her question not to Walt, but to Hannah.

She licked her too-dry lips and tried to remember something from Daniel Metwater's blog, which she had read repeatedly since Emily had announced she was joining his group. "We're tired of the shallow commercialism and focus on materialism so rampant in the modern world," she said. "We want to be a part of the community the Prophet is building—close to nature and working for the good of one another."

"It's not just a matter of camping in the wilderness for a few weeks," Starfall said. "You have to agree to contribute your resources for the good of all. And you have to work. Everyone in the Family has a job to do."

"We're not afraid of work," Walt said. "And we wouldn't expect the Prophet to take us in and provide for us without us contributing. We have money to contribute."

Starfall's unblinking gaze was starting to make Hannah nervous. She moved closer to Walt, her shoulder brushing his. "Can you arrange for us to meet the Prophet?" she asked.

Starfall's expression didn't soften, but she nodded. "You can follow us to camp when we get ready to leave here."

"Is there anything I can do to help?" Hannah asked. She turned to the first young woman. "I could hold the baby for you."

The woman put one arm protectively around the child. "He's happier with me."

"Wait for us over there or outside." Starfall pointed to the corner of the laundry.

"Come on, honey." Walt took her arm and led her to the grouping of chairs. "You need to rein it in a little," he said under his breath. "She thinks you want to kidnap her kid."

"I just wanted to verify it's really a boy. Don't you think he looks small for seven months?"

"I have no idea. I haven't spent a lot of time around babies."

She slumped into one of the molded plastic chairs grouped against the back wall. "I haven't either. Before I left to come here I read everything I could find on babies, but there's so much information out there it's impossible to absorb."

"Most new parents seem to manage fine." He patted her shoulder. "You will, too."

She studied the trio of women sorting laundry across the room. "What kind of a name is Starfall?"

"I'm not sure where Metwater's followers get their names," he said. "Maybe Metwater christens them."

"If Emily took a new name, maybe that's why no one recognized her when you asked about her."

"It's possible." He squeezed her hand. "We'll try to find out."

Odd that holding his hand felt so natural now. If he was really her husband, it was the kind of thing he would do, right? But it annoyed her that she was settling into this role so easily. She was a strong woman and she didn't need a man to make her feel safe. And she couldn't afford to lose focus on her real purpose here—to find and care for her niece.

She slid her fingers out of his grasp. "I think we should come up with a list of reasons Metwater would want us as part of his group. It makes sense that he wouldn't want a bunch of freeloaders."

"From what little we've seen, men seem to leave the group more often than women," Walt said. "So he's always in need of extra muscle."

Her gaze slid to his chest and arms. He had muscle, all right. She shifted in her chair. "It doesn't look as if he has any shortage of young women followers. I should think of something to make me look like a better possible disciple. I supposed I could offer up my bank account."

"I'll admit that would probably be an inducement, but I doubt you'll need it."

"But I ought to have something to offer," she said. "Maybe I could say I was a teacher and I could teach the children. That would be a good way to get to know the mothers, too."

"It would. But babies don't really need school yet. I think Metwater will want you in his group because you're just his type."

"His type?"

"Beautiful."

She stared at him, a blush heating her face. Not that she was naive about her looks, but to hear him say it that way caught her off guard. She glanced at the women in front of the bank of washers, noting that they were all young, slender and, yes, quite attractive. "Are you saying Metwater favors beautiful women?"

"From what I've heard, he's got a regular harem

around him all the time. The Rangers did a rough census of the group when they first moved onto park land, and there wasn't anyone out there over the age of forty, and most of them are a lot younger. Two-thirds of the group are women and a number of them are, well, stunning." He shrugged. "You should fit right in."

He probably meant that as a compliment, but his words made her uncomfortable. "I really don't like being judged by my looks—good or bad," she said. "It's something I've had to struggle against in the scientific community my whole career. There are plenty of people out there—plenty of men—who still think a pretty blonde can't possibly be smart."

"I don't think you're dumb—not by a long shot," he said. "I'm just telling you what I've observed about Metwater. If you know what you're getting into, maybe you can use his predilections to your advantage."

"You mean, pretend to be the dumb blonde so he'll be less likely to suspect me of being up to something?"

"That's one way to approach it."

She crossed her arms over her stomach. Playing down her intellect and playing up her looks went against everything she believed in. But if it would help her find Joy and bring her home safely… "I'll think about it," she said, and stood. "Right now, I'm going outside to get some fresh air."

WALT WATCHED HANNAH walk away. She nodded to the three Family members as she passed, but didn't stop to chat. He settled back in his chair, chin on his chest, pretending to nap, though he kept an eye on the three women. Hannah was ticked off about his comments about her looks. He was only stating fact, and trying to give her a hint at what she might be in for.

Not that he intended to let Daniel Metwater lay a finger on her. One more reason he was glad they had decided to pass themselves off as husband and wife instead of brother and sister. He couldn't count on the Prophet not to go after a married woman, but it might slow him down. Walt didn't intend for the two of them to be in the camp any longer than necessary. With luck, they would find Hannah's niece within a day or two and get out of Dodge.

"We're ready to leave now, if you want to follow us."

Starfall hefted a large garbage bag he presumed was full of clean laundry and started out the door. Walt hurried to catch up. "Let me take that," he said, and carried the laundry the rest of the way to the battered sedan she pointed out.

Hannah joined them beside the car. "Do you need help with anything else?" she asked.

"No." Starfall slid into the driver's seat and turned the key. "Just try to keep up."

She was already pulling out of the parking lot when Walt and Hannah reached his motorcycle. "I think she's purposely trying to lose us," Hannah said as she pulled on the helmet.

"No chance of that." He put on his own helmet and mounted the bike. "I already know where the camp is." She climbed on behind him and he started the engine. "It's going to be a rough and dusty ride once we reach the dirt roads. Nothing I can do about it."

"Despite what you might think, I'm not some delicate flower who withers if I have to deal with a little dirt," she said. "I'm tougher than I look."

He heard the steel in her voice and sensed it in her posture as she sat up straight behind him. Only her hands tightly gripping his sides gave any clue to her nervousness. He remembered the matter-of-fact way she had laid out her story in the Rangers' office, with no tears or pleadings. As much as he found himself wanting to look after her, she was a woman used to looking after herself, and she wasn't going to let him forget it.

Starfall obviously wasn't concerned about speed limits, as she drove fifteen and twenty miles over the posted speeds all the way into the park. Only when they turned onto the first dirt road did she slow down, in deference to the washboard surface of the two-track that cut across the wilderness.

The landscape that spread out around them was unlike what most people associated with Colorado. Though distant mountains showed snowcapped peaks against an expanse of turquoise sky, the land in the park and surrounding wilderness areas was high desert. Sagebrush and stunted pinyons dotted the rolling expanse of cracked brown earth, and boulders the size of cars lay scattered like thrown dice. Though the terrain looked dry and barren, it was home to vibrant life, from colorful lizards and swift rabbits to deer and black bear. Hidden springs formed lush oases, and the roaring cataract of the Gunnison River had cut the deep Black Canyon that gave the park its name, a place of wild beauty unlike any other in the United States.

Walt had to slow the Harley to a crawl to steer around the network of potholes and protruding rocks, and to avoid being choked by the sedan's dust. Even if he hadn't already known the location of Metwater's camp, the rooster tail of dust that fanned out behind the car hung in the air long after the vehicle passed, providing a clear guide to their destination.

By the time he and Hannah reached the small parking area, the women had the car unloaded and were preparing to carry the bundles of clean laundry over the footbridge. Without asking, they left two bundles behind. Walt and Hannah took these and fell into step behind them.

The camp looked much as it had on his visit four days before, people gathered in front of trailers and tents, others working around picnic tables in a large open-sided shelter with a roof made of logs and woven branches. A group of men played cards in the shade of a lean-to fashioned from a tarp, while a trio of children ran along the creek, pausing every few steps to plunge sticks into the water.

"There are a lot of people here," Hannah whispered.

"A couple dozen, best we can determine," Walt said.

A man stepped forward to take the bag of laundry from Starfall. "Who are they?" he asked, jerking his head toward Walt and Hannah.

"They want to join the Family," she said.

The man, who looked to be in his late twenties, wore his sandy hair long and pulled back in a ponytail. He had a hawk nose and a cleft in his chin, and the build of a cage fighter or a bull rider—not tall, but all stringy muscle and barely contained energy. He looked them up and down, then spat to the side. "I guess that's up to the Prophet," he said.

He and Starfall walked away, leaving Walt and Hannah standing alone on the edge of the camp. Hannah moved closer and he put his arm around her. "What do we do now?" she asked.

"Let's go talk to the Prophet."

"Where is he?" she asked.

"What's your best guess?" he asked.

She surveyed the camp, taking in the motley collection of dwellings, from a camper shell on the back of a pickup truck with one flat tire to a luxurious motor home with an array of solar panels on the roof. "My guess is the big RV," she said.

"You get an A." He took his arm from around her. "Come on. Let's see if the Prophet will grant us an interview."

No one said anything as they headed toward the motor home, but Walt could feel dozens of eyes on them. No one was rushing to welcome the new converts with open arms, that was for sure. Was it because they were waiting to take their cue from Metwater? Or had the Prophet instilled suspicion of all outsiders in his followers?

They mounted the steps to the RV and Walt rapped hard on the door. After a moment it opened and Andi Matheson answered. Andi—or Asteria, as she called herself now—had had more contact with the Rangers than anyone else in camp, but she showed no sign of recognition as she stared at Walt. "Yes?"

"We'd like to see the Prophet," he said. "We—my wife and I—" he indicated Hannah "—are big admirers of his and would like to join the group."

She nodded, as if this made perfect sense, and held the door open wider. "Come in."

The interior of the RV was dim and cool, the living room filled with a leather sofa and several upholstered chairs. Andi indicated they should sit, then disappeared through an archway into the back of the vehicle.

Walt sat on the sofa and Hannah settled next to him. She was breathing shallowly, and he could almost feel the nervousness rolling off her in waves.

He gripped her hand and squeezed. “It’s going to be okay,” he said.

She nodded, and didn’t pull away.

“The woman who let us in is Andi Matheson,” Walt said, keeping his voice low.

Hannah nodded. “I read about her online. She’s the daughter of someone famous, right?”

“Her father is Senator Pete Matheson—though right now he’s serving time for murdering an FBI agent.”

“She’s obviously pregnant,” Hannah said. “Is Metwater the father?”

“No,” Walt said. “That would be the man the senator killed.”

Hannah’s face softened with sympathy. “How terrible for her.”

“She seems to have settled in nicely with Metwater,” Walt said.

There wasn’t a clock in the room, so he had no idea how long they waited, though he thought it might have been as long as ten minutes. “What’s taking so long?” Hannah whispered.

Just then, Andi reappeared from the back of the RV. “The Prophet will see you,” she said.

Walt and Hannah stood and started toward Andi. She held up a hand. “He doesn’t want to see you together,” she said. She turned to Hannah. “He wants to interview you first. Alone.”

Chapter Five

"I don't think—" Walt began, but Hannah interrupted him.

"I don't mind talking with him by myself." She assumed what she hoped was an eager expression. "It would be a privilege to meet the Prophet." Was that laying it on too thick? Probably not, for a man who had the nerve to refer to himself as the Prophet.

Andi turned to Walt. "You can wait outside," she said. "I'll call you when it's your turn."

Walt turned to Hannah. "If you're sure?"

"I'll be fine." After all, it wasn't as if Metwater was going to do anything with Andi right here and a bunch of other people around. And it wasn't as if she hadn't had experience fending off fresh men. Even if Metwater was the lecher Walt had made him out to be, Hannah could handle him.

Walt left, then Andi put on a broad-brimmed hat and headed for the door also. "Where are you going?" Hannah asked.

"The Prophet wants to speak with you alone," she said, and left, the door clicking shut behind her.

Hannah hugged her arms across her chest and walked to the window, but heavy shades blocked any view out—or in. She took a deep breath, fighting for calm. She shouldn't be afraid of Metwater. Walt was close by if she needed anything. She needed to keep her head and use this opportunity to learn as much as possible about the Prophet, and about Emily and Joy.

"Please, have a seat. I want you to be comfortable."

She turned and stared at the man who spoke. Metwater—and this had to be Metwater—was almost naked, wearing only a pair of low-slung, loose lounge pants in some sort of silky fabric. The kind of thing she'd seen Hugh Hefner wear in old photographs. At the thought, she had to stifle a laugh.

"Please share what you find so amusing." Barefoot, he moved into the room with the sensual grace of a panther, lamplight gleaming on the smooth muscles of his chest and arms and stomach. Curly dark hair framed a face like Michelangelo's *David*, the shadow of beard adding a masculine roughness.

All mirth deserted her as he moved closer still, stopping when he was almost touching her, so that she could feel the heat of his body, smell his musk and see the individual lashes that framed his dark eyes. He stared at her, crowding her personal space, stripping away her privacy. She found it impossible to look away from that gaze—the hypnotic stare of a predator.

"What amuses you?" he asked again, his voice deep and velvety, seductive.

"I laugh when I'm nervous," she said. "I never thought I'd get to meet you in person." This much was true. She had never really wanted to meet the man she blamed for her sister's death. Even if Metwater hadn't killed Emily, Hannah believed her sister wouldn't have died if she had stayed near her real family instead of joining up with this pretend one.

"There's no need to be nervous around me." He took her hand and led her toward the sofa. She forced herself not to pull away. Better to let him think she was under his spell. He had the kind of personality that would enchant many women. She could see how Emily, pregnant and feeling alone, mourning the loss of her fiancé and the future she had planned, might fall for someone like this. She would revel in the attention of someone so charismatic and seemingly powerful. She wouldn't have seen through his charm the way Hannah did.

She slid her hand out of his grasp and sat up straight, hoping her prim posture would put him off a little. The dimples on either side of his mouth deepened and he leaned toward her. "Tell me why you're interested in becoming a member of my family," he said.

His family. Not "our family" or "the family", but

something that belonged to him. "My husband and I want to build a life that focuses on essentials—what's really important." That was a quote straight out of his blog.

"Why not do as so many others have done and set up a homestead on your own, or sell everything and take to the road?" he asked. "You could sign up for missionary work overseas or join a religious order. Why come to me?"

"While we believe in spirituality, we don't belong to any particular religion," she said. "And we want to work together with a like-minded group with an inspiring leader." Because, obviously, it was all about him.

"We don't have many married couples here," he said. "We discourage it, in fact."

"Why is that?" She knew he wanted her to ask the question.

"I see marriage as an outdated construct," he said. "And it's a distraction. How can you pledge loyalty to the Family as a whole when you've already pledged yourself to one other person? A single person is much freer to follow the dictates of her heart."

"So you require your followers to be single?" she asked.

"Not at all." He brushed his fingers across her shoulder. "I merely see it as a preferable state."

She shifted, putting a few more inches between them—the most she could manage.

"How did you learn about me?" he asked.

Walt had instructed her to say she had discovered the Prophet's blog online and that had led to the two of them reading everything they could find about him and his disciples. But she couldn't pass up the chance to learn more about his connection with her sister. "A friend told me about you," she said. "Before she left to join your group. I'm hoping she's still here. I would love to reconnect with her."

"What is your friend's name?"

"Emily Dietrich."

His expression didn't change, but something flickered in his eyes—a darkness he quickly masked. "Your friend told you she was going to join the Family?"

"Yes. I'm sure that's what she said. She attended a rally where you spoke and was convinced you offered exactly what she was looking for, for herself and her baby. Is she here? When can I see her?"

He took her hand again, holding on tightly when she tried to pull free. "When was the last time you spoke to your friend?" he asked.

"About six months ago, right before she left to follow you." *Stick to the truth as much as possible*, Walt had told her.

"Your friend must have changed her mind," he said. "She never came to me. At least, no one using the name Emily Dietrich has ever been a member of my family."

He sounded sincere, but the flash of irritation she had seen at the first mention of Emily's name told her he was lying. He had recognized the name, and didn't like that she had brought it up. "How odd," she said. "I wonder what happened to her?"

"Does it change your mind about joining us, knowing your friend isn't here?" he asked.

"Of course not," she said. "You asked how I learned about you, and it was through her. I was hoping I'd get to see her again, but she isn't the main reason we're here. It's because we believe in everything you teach and we want that kind of life for ourselves."

"Do you know what it means to be a part of a family?" he asked.

"Well, I suppose..." She hesitated, trying to remember what he had said about this in his writings, but she was drawing a blank. "Family members look out for and support one another," she said. "You try to live in harmony and act in a way that's to the benefit of everyone, not simply yourself."

"True." He nodded. "As a part of my family, I would expect you to put the needs of the group ahead of yourself. We purposely separate ourselves from the outside world in order to focus on perfecting our union. While I would never forbid you to be in contact with relatives and friends from your old life, most people find as they immerse themselves in the day-to-day life of the Family, they are less and less inclined to want to be with others who don't share our sense of purpose and our views."

She tried to look thoughtful. "I can see that," she said.

He rubbed his thumb up and down the third finger of her left hand. "You said you were married. Where is your ring?"

She stared down at her empty fingers. She and Walt had spent hours going over all the details of coming here. Why hadn't they remembered a ring? "We don't hold with the trappings of society. We don't need a band of precious metal to seal our vows to one another."

He gave her hand a final squeeze—so hard she winced—then released his grip on her and sat back. He was no longer the seducing lover, but the practical businessman. "What resources do you bring to the group?" he said. "Everyone must contribute for the good of the whole."

"We have some money, from savings and from selling some things to pay for our trip here," she said. "And I enjoy working with children. I can teach the older ones and help care for younger ones."

"What about your husband? What does he do?"

They had rehearsed this. What had Walt said? "He was a carpenter. He's very good with his hands."

"Oh, is he?" Why did the words sound so sarcastic? "You'll have to provide your own shelter and clothing," he said. "Everyone here has to earn his or her keep. You'll be expected to embark on a course of study until you prove yourself ready to join us."

"What will we study?" she asked.

"Whatever I deem necessary." He rested his hand on her shoulder, a heavy, possessive touch that had her fighting her instinct to pull away. "I will personally instruct you on what you need to know to be a good disciple."

"Walt and I will look forward to learning more," she said.

"It's important for you to maintain your individuality, even though you are married," he said. "I consider you and your husband two separate candidates for inclusion in our group. Not everyone earns full acceptance as a member of the Family. You'll come to see the benefit of this as part of your teaching."

"Do you ever kick anyone out?" she asked. "I mean, if they do something that upsets the harmony of the group?" Had Emily done something to upset him? Is that why she had been so afraid?

"We punish when necessary. Our justice is not the justice of the world. We answer to a higher power."

"What does that mean?" It sounded as if he thought he was above the law, free to act in whatever way he wished. No wonder Emily had been afraid.

"You'll learn as part of your training." He took her hand and pulled her to her feet. "Come. It's time for you to meet your future sisters and brothers."

"What about Walt?"

"Don't worry about him. I'll see that he's taken care of."

She wasn't sure she liked the sound of that. He had made it clear he didn't think too much of marriage—and the implication was that he preferred to focus on her and leave Walt out in the cold. She definitely didn't like the possessive way he held her hand—she had always resented men who tried to take over and drag her around like some pretty ornament who was supposed to smile and look nice, but not express too many opinions. She managed to pull her hand from his grasp. But she hastened to soothe the affront that flashed in his eyes with a smile and flattering words. "I'm thrilled you've taken such an interest," she said. "I never dreamed I'd be so privileged as to study with you personally."

He put one arm around her and pulled her close. "You and I are going to be good friends," he said, and pressed his lips to her cheek. "Very special friends."

WALT DIDN'T HAVE to spend very long in the Family's camp to confirm a few things the other Rangers had told him about Daniel Metwater. The Prophet had surrounded himself with mostly young people and mostly women. Beautiful women. Every woman Walt encountered was strikingly attractive. Hannah would fit in perfectly with the rest of Metwater's harem—the thought made Walt's jaw tighten. He told himself if she was a trained officer, instead of a civilian, he wouldn't be so agitated about her being in that RV alone with the self-proclaimed prophet. The sooner they learned what they needed to know about Hannah's sister and niece, the sooner they could get out of here.

He could feel the other Family members watching him as he stood outside the RV, the sun beating down, making him sweat. He wiped his brow, then strode over to the card players. They looked up and watched his approach, expressions wary. "Hey," he said, nodding in greeting. "My name's Walt. My wife and I are hoping to join the Family."

The stocky, bearded man who had greeted Walt and Marco when they had previously visited the camp looked him up and down, but gave no indication he recognized him. "I saw you ride in," he said. "Nice-looking bike."

"Nice-looking wife, too." A lanky blond laid his cards facedown on the blanket they were sitting around. "The Prophet will like her."

A couple of the other men snickered. Walt ignored them. "Good to meet you."

He offered his hand to the blond, who shook it. "I'm Jobie. This is Emerson." He indicated the man next to him, who wore black-rimmed glasses and a panama hat. "That's Kiram." He nodded to the bearded man.

Walt acknowledged each man in turn. Emerson

offered his hand to shake, but Kiram only regarded him coolly.

"The camp looks pretty nice," Walt said. "It's a good location, you've got time to play cards, nobody hassling you."

"It's okay." Kiram laid aside his cards also and nodded to an empty space across from him. "Have a seat."

"Thanks." Walt lowered himself to the blanket. "How long have you been following the Prophet?" he asked.

"A while."

"Kiram's been with the Family practically from the beginning," Jobie said. "You got any cigs?"

"Sorry," Walt said. "I don't smoke."

"Smoking isn't allowed in camp," Kiram said.

Jobie scowled at him. "I didn't say I was going to smoke it in camp."

"I guess there are a lot of rules you have to follow," Walt said. "I know I read on the Prophet's blog that he doesn't allow guns in the camp or anything." An injunction Walt had ignored. He considered the pistol he wore in an ankle holster as one more way to protect himself and Hannah out here in the wilderness.

"There are rules," Kiram said. "It wouldn't say much about a group that preaches peace to have us all walking around armed."

"I can see that," Walt said.

"Was it your wife's idea to join up or yours?" Emerson asked.

"We decided together," Walt said.

"My girlfriend talked me into it," Emerson said. He nudged his hat farther back on his head. "We thought it would be cool living together with a bunch of people who thought the same way we did, communing with nature, hanging out in the woods and living off the land."

"And is it?" Walt asked. "Cool, I mean."

Emerson glanced toward Kiram, who was studying him, expressionless. "Sometimes," he said. "I guess no life is perfect. My girlfriend likes it well enough."

Jobie leaned toward Walt. "The thing you need to know about this place is that the women run the show. Well, the Prophet runs everything, but mostly, he runs the women."

"So you're telling me a woman can get away with anything around here," Walt said.

Jobie shook his head. "Even the women have lines they can't cross," he said. "If they displease the Prophet, then they're out of here. Doesn't happen often, but sometimes..." His voice trailed away and he picked up his hand of cards again.

Though the words weren't particularly ominous, something in Jobie's tone sent a chill up Walt's spine. "A girl I went to school with used to talk about joining up with the Family," he said. "I wonder if she ever did. Her name was Emily Dietrich."

"A lot of people here take on a new name," Jobie said. "Or they just go by one name."

"This girl was blonde, with blue eyes. Really pretty." Which essentially described Hannah. The picture Hannah had shown him left little doubt that the two were sisters.

Jobie and Emerson looked at each other. "Was that the woman who was here in the spring for a while?" Jobie asked. "It kind of sounds like her."

"That wasn't her." Kiram didn't look up from his cards when he spoke, but Walt sensed the man was focused on the conversation.

Jobie shrugged. "Guess not, then. Maybe she changed her mind about joining up. I'd probably remember her if she had. There aren't that many of us, and I tend to remember the women, especially." He grinned.

"What happened to the woman who was here in the spring?" Walt directed his question to Kiram.

Still holding his cards, Kiram stood. "If you want to get along here, you need to learn not to ask so many questions," he said.

He walked away. Walt turned to the other two. "What's his problem?"

"He's got a point," Emerson said. "Asking questions is a good way to get into trouble around here."

"What kind of trouble?" Walt asked.

The two exchanged looks. "The Prophet punishes the disobedient."

"What kind of punishment?" Walt pressed.

"Just keep your mouth shut and you won't have to find out." Jobie nodded toward the motor home. "Here comes your wife."

Hannah exited the RV with Metwater at her side. The Prophet had one arm around her shoulders. She was smiling, but Walt sensed tension. "Everyone, I have an announcement to make," Metwater said.

Everyone around Walt put aside whatever they were doing and moved toward the RV. Even the children stopped playing and ran to their mothers' sides to stare up at Metwater. It was as if he had brainwashed them all into thinking he really was a prophet, Walt thought, as he pushed through the crowd to the bottom of the steps. Hannah met his gaze, but Metwater ignored him.

"I'd like you to meet a new candidate for membership into the Family," Metwater announced, in a deep, rich voice that carried easily over the crowd. He smiled at Hannah and squeezed her shoulder. "I think we'll call you Serenity."

"Oh." Her smile faded. "I really prefer my own name," she said.

"Serenity suits you," he said. He turned back to the crowd. "Say hello to Serenity, everyone."

"Hello, Serenity," they chorused.

Hannah frowned, but said nothing. Walt mounted the steps, brushing aside the one man who moved forward as if to stop him. He moved to Hannah's side and put his arm around her.

"This is Walter," Metwater said. "He came to us with Serenity."

"Hannah is my wife," he said. "And it's Walt, not Walter." His grandmother was the only one who ever called him Walter.

The dreadlocked blond who had taken the laundry bag from Starfall ran toward them, a little out of breath. "The cops are back," he said.

Metwater looked over the crowd, to the path that led into camp. Sure enough, Rangers Michael Dance and Lance Carpenter were making their way down the trail. Obviously, Carpenter had made it back from his honeymoon and Dance had returned from Denver, but what were the two officers doing here?

Dance and Carpenter stopped at the edge of the clearing and looked the crowd over. Walt took Hannah's hand and tugged her toward the steps, planning to melt into the background. He figured his fellow officers were savvy enough not to give him away, but he didn't want to risk anyone—especially Metwater—picking up on any subtle cues that they knew each other.

"We've had a report of a young woman who went missing from Montrose a couple of days ago," Dance said. His voice didn't have the orator's tones of Metwater, but it carried well over the crowd. "A witness thought they saw her hitchhiking near here and we wondered if anyone here has seen her." He consulted his phone's screen. "She's described as five feet six inches tall, with short black hair, olive skin and brown eyes. Her name is Lucia Raton."

"We don't know anything about this missing girl," Metwater said. "Why would you assume we would?"

"She might have left her home intending to join your group," Lance said. "Or if she was lost, she might have wandered to your camp looking for help."

"These are the only people new to our camp," Metwater said. "And as you can see, neither of them fit your description of this girl."

Walt realized that Metwater was pointed to him and Hannah, and that everyone—including the two Rangers—had turned to look at them.

Lance frowned. "Hey, Walt," he said. "What are you doing here?"

Chapter Six

Hannah tightened her grip on Walt's hand. Nothing like having a cop call you out to arouse suspicion in a group of people you were lying to. Walt had tensed up and was all but glaring at the Ranger.

"I think these are the two who stopped me and gave me a ticket day before yesterday," he said. His glower looked real enough to Hannah—he was probably furious at his coworkers for blowing his cover.

The taller of the two Rangers nudged his partner. "Should have figured his type would show up with this bunch," he said.

Hannah saw the moment the first Ranger—his name badge said Carpenter—clicked to what was going on. He moved to stand in front of Walt. "Do you know anything about this missing woman?" he asked. "Maybe you gave her a ride on your bike?"

"I only have room for one woman on my bike," Walt said, and pulled Hannah closer. "You remember my wife, Hannah, don't you, Officer?"

If Carpenter was surprised to learn that Walt suddenly had a wife, his sunglasses helped hide his reaction. "She's not the kind of woman a man forgets," he said. He held up his cell phone, which showed a picture of a round-faced, dark-haired woman who couldn't be very far out of her teens. "Have either of you seen this girl?"

Hannah shook her head.

"Why do you people automatically assume we're responsible for anything that goes wrong?" Metwater moved in behind them. "We are a peaceful people and you've never found any evidence to contradict that, yet you continue to harass us."

"In this case, Lucia's parents found your blog bookmarked on her computer." The taller officer, Dance, joined them. He focused on Metwater, avoiding looking at Hannah or Walt.

"That doesn't make us guilty of anything," Metwater said.

"No, it doesn't," Dance agreed. "But we're talking about a missing woman. We have to check out every possible lead. We're questioning a lot of people, and you're one of them."

"So, you don't know anything about Lucia Raton?" Carpenter asked. "You haven't seen her or heard from her?"

"No, I haven't." Metwater spread his arms wide. "Look around you, officer. The camp isn't that large. It's not as if someone could sneak in here without my knowing about it."

"Do you get people stopping by often, wanting to join up?" Dance glanced at Hannah.

"Occasionally," Metwater said. "My message touches people. They want to be a part of what I'm building here."

"What exactly are you building?" Carpenter frowned at the haphazard collection of tents, shanties and trailers.

"A community of peace and cooperation."

Were they really as peaceful as Metwater wanted everyone to believe? Hannah wondered. Metwater's charisma could only go so far in controlling his followers. Did he use other methods to keep everyone in line—methods that had frightened Emily, and maybe even led to her death?

"Let us know if you hear or see anything that might help us find this woman," Dance said. "Her family is very worried."

Metwater inclined his head, like a king deigning to notice a subject. Dance and Carpenter left. Walt took Hannah's hand. "Come on," he said. "We'd better find a place to set up our tent."

WALT HADN'T TAKEN a step when a strong hand gripped his shoulder. "What was that all about?" Metwater asked, his voice a low growl.

Walt played dumb. "What was what all about?"

"That officer recognized you. He greeted you by name."

"He was just giving me a hard time, the way he

did when he gave us that ticket. You know how those cops are."

Metwater's eyes narrowed. "I would have thought the Rangers had better things to do than to give out speeding tickets."

"I guess he just wanted to hassle me—the way he did you."

Metwater nodded, though the suspicion didn't leave his eyes. "Tomorrow you can begin your training," he said.

"Training?" Hannah didn't look happy about this prospect.

"I will instruct you in preparation for you being accepted as full members of the Family," Metwater said.

"Okay." Walt hid his annoyance at the prospect. All he wanted was to find Hannah's niece and leave. He couldn't say if Metwater was guilty of breaking any laws, but Walt disliked pretty much everything about him, from his snake-oil salesman charm to his glib new age pontificating.

"It's time to eat," Metwater said. He took Hannah's hand in his. "We'll share a meal and gather by the fire. You can begin to learn our ways."

Walt moved to Hannah's side and took her other hand. Now that they were embedded with Metwater and his group, he realized he would need to add another job to his list of duties. In addition to locating Hannah's niece and finding out more about her sister's death, he would need to keep a close eye on his pretend wife, to keep her out of the Prophet's clutches.

It was after ten before Walt and Hannah had the chance to break away from the group. Dinner had consisted of decent stew and bread. Afterward, everyone had gathered around a campfire to witness what Metwater explained was a spiritual dance but what looked to Walt like two scantily clad women performing for Metwater. The man himself stayed glued to Hannah's side until the evening's festivities ended. "You're welcome to stay in my RV," he told her as she and Walt prepared to leave. "You'll be much more comfortable there."

Walt bristled and was about to remind Metwater that Hannah was his wife and therefore her place was with him when she stepped between them. "Thank you," she said, with a sweet smile for Metwater. "That's so considerate of you, but I'll be fine in the tent with Walt." Then she took Walt's hand and led him away.

"He's got a lot of nerve," Walt fumed. "Propositioning you with me standing right there."

"It wasn't exactly a proposition," she said. "And there's no need for you to go all caveman. I know how to look after myself."

"Sorry." He winced inwardly, realizing how the words he had almost said would have sounded to her. It wasn't his place to tell her where she belonged—even if they had been truly married. "He just rubs me the wrong way."

"He knows that and he uses it to his advantage."

They retrieved the tent and two sleeping bags from

the motorcycle. "We should set up away from everyone else," Walt said. "Less chance of being overheard or spied on."

"Do you think Metwater suspects something?" she asked.

"I think he's the type who suspects everyone. I'm no expert on groups like this, but I've done a little reading. The best way for one man to control a group of diverse people is to have a team of enforcers whose job is to report back to the leader about what everyone else is up to. Those people get to make sure everyone else obeys all the rules and doesn't get out of line."

"Who are Metwater's enforcers?" she asked.

"I met one guy who fits the bill," Walt said. "A big, bearded man who goes by the name of Kiram. Apparently he's been with Metwater a long time, and the others seem wary of him. There are probably one or two others."

"What happens if someone breaks a rule?" she asked.

"I don't know. But I intend to find out." They had reached the edge of the camp, at a point farthest from Metwater's RV, and farthest from the trail that led into the clearing. Walt shone his flashlight on a large, leaning juniper. "How about here, under this tree?" he asked. "We'd be out of the way and have some shade in the daytime."

"Sure." She unzipped the tent bag and pulled out the stiff bundle of green-and-black polyester. "Why did that officer, Carpenter, call you out this afternoon?" she asked. "He could have ruined everything."

"Lance just got back from his honeymoon. And Michael was on assignment in another part of the state." He began fitting the shock-corded tent poles together. "My guess is the missing persons call came in and they decided to check out the camp without checking in with headquarters, and no one had briefed them. It worked out okay, though. I think Metwater believed my story about the ticket."

"What do you think this training is going to consist of?"

"I don't know, but maybe we'll get lucky and won't have to endure it for long." He laid aside the completed poles and looked at her. "What happened in the RV this afternoon after I was escorted out?" he asked.

She made a face. "He asked how we heard about him, why we wanted to join up—about what you'd expect."

"Did he make a pass at you?"

She laughed.

"What's so funny?" he asked.

"It's just not a question I expected."

"Well, did he? He was certainly leering at you enough."

"No, he didn't make a pass at me. Not exactly."

"Did he or didn't he?"

She shrugged. "He put his arm around me. He said he thought marriage was an outmoded concept."

"He would just as soon get rid of me and have you stay to be one of his faithful female followers."

"Are you jealous?" She wasn't laughing anymore—instead her blue eyes searched his, making him feel a little too vulnerable.

"I'm not jealous," he said. "But I don't trust Metwater. He clearly has a lot of beautiful women hovering around him, and I think he sees you as another one."

"No chance of that," she said. "I've never been attracted to men who think they're God's gift to women."

What kind of man are *you attracted to?* he wondered, but pushed the thought aside. He didn't have the best track record with women and he ought to be focusing on the job at hand. "I don't trust all his talk of living peacefully and promoting harmony," he said. "That's not the impression I got when I talked to some of the men."

"What did you find out?"

"They didn't say anything specific, but they hinted that people who didn't follow Metwater's rules—or people who asked too many questions—were punished."

"He said something to me about punishment, too," she said. "That they had their own rules and answered to a higher power—which I interpreted as another way of saying he thinks he's above the law. Did you get any idea of what kind of punishment they use? He wouldn't tell me."

"The men I was talking to wouldn't say, either. And they changed the subject when I tried to find out more. But when I mentioned Emily, I got the impression at least a couple of them knew who I was talking about, though they pretended not to."

"You asked about Emily?" She clutched his wrist. "What did you say? What did they say?"

"One of the men said he thought she had been here in the spring. Does that sound about right?"

"Yes. That would have been about the time she left home to follow Metwater. The first letter she sent me arrived in May." She bent and began threading the poles into the channel across the top of the tent. "I asked Metwater about her, too."

He froze. "I thought we agreed you weren't going to say anything about her."

"I couldn't pass up the chance to learn about her. I didn't say she was my sister—I told him she was a friend."

"What did he say?"

"He said he'd never heard of her. But I think he was lying."

"I'm going to try to find out more, but we have to be careful asking questions." He slid the pole into the other channel of the tent, and together they tilted the structure upright. "You try to make friends with the women and find out what you can about your niece—though you realize she may not be here."

"I know. But I feel like she is."

He began hammering in stakes to secure the tent. "You can go ahead and go inside and get ready for bed," he said. "I'll join you in a minute."

"All right." She crawled into the tent and zipped it up after her.

Walt pounded the stakes in with a mallet, hitting them harder than necessary, working off some of his frustration. He needed to get a grip on his feelings before he crawled into that tent to spend the night with Hannah. He had thought pretending to be her husband would be just another undercover gig, one that he would handle professionally. But being this close to her, seeing Metwater leer at her, had triggered something primitive in him—a possessiveness and desire to protect her that caught him off guard.

Now they had a long night ahead of them in a small tent. He couldn't let himself be the man who was attracted to a smart, beautiful woman. He had to be a cop with a job to do—and that job didn't include letting emotion get the better of his good sense.

HANNAH HUDDLED IN a sleeping bag on one side of the tent and waited for Walt to come in. She had changed under the covers, wishing she had opted for sleepwear that wasn't quite so revealing. At the time she had packed, she hadn't been thinking about the fact that she'd be spending the nights alone with Walt. She had pictured them sleeping in a cabin or a travel trailer, not a small tent with only inches separating them.

The tent zipper slid open and Walt crawled in, flashlight illuminating the interior. "Comfortable?" he asked.

"It's not too bad," she lied. She had never slept on the ground like this before—had never realized it could be so hard.

He crawled to the other sleeping bag and began removing his boots. Boots off, he pulled his shirt off over his head. She closed her eyes, but not before she caught a glimpse of his lean, muscular body and felt the instant jolt of arousal.

The light went out and darkness closed around them, so that Walt was only a denser shadow across from her, though in the small space she could hear his breathing, and take in the spice-and-sweat scent of him. She felt the heat of his presence beside her, more intimate somehow than if they had been touching. The idea made her heart race, and she kneaded her hands on her thighs, listening to the sounds of him finishing undressing—the lowering of a zipper and the soft hush of cloth being shoved down, then the crisper rustle of the sleeping bag as he crawled inside. "At least we don't have to worry about it getting really cold at night," he said.

"I've never been camping before," she said.

"Never?"

She shook her head, then realized he couldn't see her. "I guess I've always been a city girl."

"It can be fun," he said. "I've spent the night in a tent in some beautiful spots all over the country."

"I guess it's different when you're by yourself," she said. "Not with a group like this, with other people all around you."

"Camping's nice with one other person," he said. "The right person."

"Did you and your girlfriend go camping?" she asked.

"Once. She didn't like it. Maybe that should have been my first clue things weren't going to work out."

"Relationships are hard," she said. "We don't always know who to trust."

"Sometimes the hardest part is trusting yourself."

"What do you mean?" She rolled onto her side to face him. She could almost make out his features in the dim light.

"I didn't pay attention when my gut told me something was off between me and my girlfriend," he said. "I didn't trust my own instincts, but I should have."

"I guess we all doubt ourselves from time to time," she said. She certainly wasn't one to give advice on handling relationships. She'd done a lousy job of that in her own life. She hadn't even been able to keep her own sister close, much less a lover.

"You're doing great so far," he said. "Just keep it

up and we'll get out of here as soon as we can." He rolled over to face the wall. "Good night."

"Good night," she said, but didn't close her eyes. Even though she longed to find her niece and leave Metwater's camp as soon as possible, she was going to miss Walt. She was going to miss lying beside him like this, pretending that in another life, they might have been a real couple, camping together because they wanted to, not because circumstance had forced them together into a relationship that felt so real, but wasn't.

"SERENITY!"

Hannah and Walt were shaking out their sleeping bags the next morning when they turned to see a pale woman moving toward them. Her hair was so blond it was almost white, and despite the intense sun here in the wilderness, her skin seemed almost devoid of color. Even her eyes were pale, a silvery gray that added to her ethereal appearance. "My name is Phoenix," she said. "I came to fetch you to come help us prepare breakfast."

"Call me Hannah. I prefer it." She rose and brushed off her skirt. "I'm happy to come and help."

Phoenix turned to Walt. "You can gather firewood. Now that we've been here awhile, the best wood is farther away and harder to haul."

"Sure." He rose also. "I'm happy to help."

"It's your job to help if you want to be one of us."

Phoenix grabbed Hannah's hand and tugged her, with enough force that Hannah stumbled, then had to hurry to keep up as Phoenix led her back toward the center of camp.

"She's right. Your job is to work for the good of the Family."

He whirled to find Kiram standing behind the tent, next to the tree trunk. He held a long-bladed knife—the kind hunters used for skinning animals. How long had he been lurking back there, listening in on Walt and Hannah's conversation? Walt forced himself to remain passive. "I thought no weapons were allowed in camp," he said.

"This knife is for ceremonial purposes," Kiram said. "And I use it for hunting." He moved away from the tree and walked around the side of the tent, studying it. "Why did you decide to camp back here, far away from everything and everyone?" He stopped beside Walt—close enough to lash out with that knife.

Walt bent and picked up the mallet he had been using to drive in stakes. He felt better with a weapon of his own, feeble as it might be against the knife. He didn't want to risk drawing the gun he wore in an ankle holster unless he absolutely had to. "We're newlyweds," he said. "We like our privacy."

"There's no such thing as privacy in a camp like this," Kiram said. "There's always someone watching you, listening to you. Before very long, everyone will know all your secrets."

Walt knew a threat when he heard one. He met Kiram's cold stare with a hard look of his own. "What's your secret?" he asked. "Why do you feel the need to sneak around in the woods with that big knife?"

"I already told you it isn't a good idea to ask too many questions." Kiram thrust the knife into the scabbard at his side.

"You told me, but you didn't tell me why. Questions can be a good way to learn things I need to know."

"People who ask questions have to be punished," Kiram said. He looked Walt up and down, as if taking his measure.

"I guess that's for the Prophet to decide, not you."

"The Prophet decides," Kiram said. "Then I do his will." He shoved past Walt, then paused a few steps away and looked back. "You didn't ask me what I was hunting."

"Why should I care what you do?" Walt said.

Kiram grinned, showing crooked bottom teeth. "I hunt rats. It's my job to keep them under control." He turned back around and strode away, leaving Walt to stare after him, gripping the mallet at his side, cold sweat beading on the back of his neck.

Chapter Seven

Hannah let Phoenix drag her to the center of the camp, where three other women were already working at two long picnic tables set up beneath a shelter fashioned of logs and branches. One table served as a prep area for the morning's meal, while the other table held two propane-fueled cooking stoves, on which bubbled two large stockpots full of oatmeal. "This is Serenity," Phoenix said by way of introduction. She handed Hannah a paring knife. "You can peel the potatoes." She indicated a ten-pound bag of potatoes at the end of the table.

"Call me Hannah," Hannah said.

"The Prophet named her Serenity," Phoenix said, and moved to stir one of the cooking pots.

"He must like you, if he gave you a name already." Starfall said. Tears streamed down her face from the onions she was chopping. She nodded to the pregnant woman across from her—Andi Matheson. "This is Asteria. And the redhead over there is Sarah."

"It's good to meet you," Hannah said. "And I am

flattered that the Prophet would give me a name, but I don't feel like a Serenity. I'm just—Hannah."

"I don't care what you call yourself, as long as you peel those potatoes." Phoenix added salt to the pot and stirred. "We need them to fry up with the onions."

Hannah picked up the knife and a potato. "Does everyone eat all their meals together?" she asked.

"Usually," Starfall said. "It's more efficient that way, and it fosters a sense of family." She swept chopped onion into a bowl and picked up another onion.

"We take turns cooking and watching the children," Asteria said. "The work is easier with more people to do it."

"I love children," Hannah said. "How many are there in camp?"

"Gloria has a five-year-old son," Asteria said. "Starfall has a son, who's seven months old. Solitude has a three-year-old, too. A boy. Zoe has six-year-old twins. And Phoenix has a fourteen-year-old daughter and a baby girl."

"My husband and I knew this was a good place to be when we saw so many children," Hannah said. The word "husband" sounded odd to her ears, but it was easy enough to say, even though she had never thought of herself as very good at lying.

"That's a good-looking man you have," Sarah said.

"Um, thanks." Hannah wasn't sure how to respond to this comment. Walt was handsome, but it wasn't as if she could claim responsibility for that. "He's a good man." She thought that much was true, at least.

"Maybe he'll be one of the rare ones who stick," Starfall said.

"What do you mean?" Hannah dropped a peeled potato into the empty pot Asteria had set in front of her and picked up another.

"A lot of guys don't adapt well to life in the Family," Asteria explained. "We have a few who have been here awhile, but a lot of them end up leaving after a few months or weeks because it's not what they expected."

"It's not a lifestyle for everyone," Phoenix said. "But the Prophet changes lives. I'm proof of that." She moved one of the pots off a burner and set another in its place.

"Mom, I need a bottle for Vicki." A lanky teenage girl, her long brown hair in pigtails, raced up to Phoenix. Dressed in shorts and a T-shirt, she looked like any other young teen, except for the baby on her hip. The infant, dressed in a pink sleeper, gurgled happily as the girl hoisted her up higher.

"Give me a minute." Phoenix added salt to the pot in front of her and tasted.

"She's been really fussy," the girl said. "I think she's hungry."

"All right." Phoenix set aside the spoon she'd been using to stir and walked to the row of coolers along the shadiest side of the shelter.

Hannah moved around the table to where the girl stood. "I'm Hannah," she said. "I'm new here."

"I'm Sophie, and this is Vicki." Sophie hitched the baby up again. "Well, her name's really Victory, but no one calls her that, except the Prophet."

"How old is she?" Hannah had to restrain herself from reaching for the infant, who kicked her little legs and waved her chubby arms, letting out a wail of protest.

"Almost four months. Would you like to hold her?"

Before Hannah could even form an answer the girl was putting the baby in her arms. Hannah cradled the child against her, patting her back and delighting in her chubby sweetness. The child quieted and stared up at Hannah with wide blue eyes.

Emily's eyes. The recognition hit Hannah like a slap. She touched one finger to the tiny dent in the baby's chin. Hannah had a dent like that in her own chin.

"She must like you. She's not usually that good with strangers." Phoenix had returned and stood at Hannah's elbow, a baby bottle in one hand.

When she leaned in to take the baby, Hannah's first instinct was to hold on tight. She could run away, find Walt and they could leave on his motorcycle. They could reach Ranger headquarters before anyone would have time to pursue them.

Logic—and probably all the lectures she had endured from Walt and his boss about needing proof that any child she found in the camp really was Emily's baby—made her reluctantly release the child to Phoenix. "You don't breast-feed?" she asked as the child latched on to the bottle.

Phoenix frowned at her. "I couldn't. I got sick right after she was born and lost my milk."

"I'm sorry," Hannah said. "That was a terribly rude question. I'm just so curious about anything to do with babies these days."

Phoenix's expression softened. "I understand." She smiled down at the baby. "I never thought I'd have another little one and now I have her. She's been a special blessing in my life."

Hannah clenched her jaw, fighting back the questions she wanted to ask. Who was this baby's father? When had she been born? Where had she been born? Did Phoenix know a woman named Emily? Instead, she held her tongue and returned to peeling potatoes, her mind working furiously. She had to find a way to prove that little Vicki wasn't Phoenix's child, but Emily's. Maybe Phoenix had taken over care of the baby because no one else was available at the time of Emily's death. Hannah was grateful to her if that was the case. But if that was so, why pass the baby off as her own? And surely she hadn't taken in the baby without Daniel Metwater's knowledge. So why had the Prophet lied about having Joy with him?

"Did you hear what those cops said about that

missing girl?" Sarah heaved a large watermelon onto the table and plunged a knife into it.

"She never should have left camp," Asteria said. "She would have been safe here."

Hannah almost dropped her potato. "You mean the girl the police were looking for was here?"

"For less than a day." Starfall scraped the last of the chopped onions into a pot. "The Prophet told her she couldn't stay, since she was underage, and she left."

"Why didn't anyone tell the Rangers that?" Hannah asked.

"One thing you need to learn if you stay here is that we don't speak to the cops," Starfall said. "It's one of the Prophet's rules."

"But if it would help them find her, why not say something?" Hannah asked. "Her poor parents must be worried sick."

"It won't help her, and it will only focus unnecessary attention on us," Starfall said. "The point is, she's not here now, and no one in the Family had anything to do with her disappearance, so the cops should look elsewhere instead of hassling us."

"Don't you go saying anything to anyone," Phoenix said. "It will only cause trouble. You don't want to start out like that."

Why would any reasonable person want to be a part of a group that hid evidence from the police? Hannah thought, but she only nodded and went back to peeling potatoes. She would have so much to tell Walt tonight—not only this bit of news about the missing young woman, but that she was sure she had found her sister's baby. All she needed was a little proof.

WALT SET OUT with Jobie and a guy who introduced himself as Slate to gather firewood. They had one hand ax and a rusting bow saw between them, and apparently Jobie and Slate had never been Boy Scouts, because they seemed to have no clue what actually made good firewood.

"I don't think that rotten stuff is going to burn very well," Walt said as Slate tugged at a fallen tree trunk that was so rotten it was growing a healthy crop of mushrooms.

The log crumbled as soon as he tried to lift it. "Guess not," he said, and straightened.

"Do you do this every day?" Walt asked.

"Pretty much," Jobie said. "We keep telling the Prophet if we had a chain saw we could cut a bunch at once and not have to work so hard, but he says the noise would draw the wrong kind of attention."

"Yeah, the cops have already got it in for us," Slate said. "They're always around here hassling us."

"Why do you think that is?" Walt asked.

"Because they're suspicious of anyone who colors outside the lines," Slate said.

"We don't bother anybody and we ask the same of

them." Jobie tugged on the end of a branch that lay beneath a tree and held up a four-foot length of juniper. He grinned and added it to his pile.

"What do we need all this wood for, anyway?" Walt asked. "Do the women cook over a fire?"

"They mostly use the camp stoves for cooking," Jobie said. "But every night after supper we have a campfire. Sometimes there's singing or dancing, like last night. Sometimes the Prophet has a message for us, and sometimes there's a ceremony."

"What kind of ceremony?" Walt asked.

"Oh, you know, like when new members join or if the Prophet has had a vision that tells him we need to perform some kind of ritual."

"You mean like saying prayers or something?"

"Not that, so much," Slate said. "Cooler stuff. Once we did fire walking, and another time everyone had to bring something to burn that represented stuff they were letting go of."

"The Prophet is really big on letting go of the past," Jobie said. "Like, if you've made mistakes or whatever, none of that has to hold you back now."

"That's what makes being part of the Family so great," Slate said. "Nobody judges you based on what you did before. You start over clean. That's why I chose the name I did. I'm a clean Slate."

Walt had read Metwater's writings about new beginnings and fresh starts. But he wondered if those teachings might not have a special appeal for people who wanted to get away with bad behavior with no consequences. Simply join up with the Prophet and all your sins are forgiven. You could get away with anything—maybe even murder.

Walt figured this wasn't the time to share his skepticism about the Prophet's message. "I guess that takes lots of firewood," he said.

"Yeah." Jobie swung the ax ineffectually at the spindly branch of a pinyon. "The Rangers think we relocated our camp because our permit expired, but really, it was just that we ran out of firewood."

Walt joined in their laughter and led the way to the next clump of scrubby trees. He estimated they were about a mile from camp, in a part of the Curecanti wilderness that he had never visited. Probably very few people came to this roadless site. "Do you ever run into wild animals out here?" he asked. "Bears or mountain lions or anything like that?"

"Sometimes we see coyotes," Jobie said. "And lots of rabbits."

"We've found other weird stuff, though," Slate said. "An old junk car, shot full of holes. A whole skeleton of some big animal, like a horse or something."

"Once we found a sofa, just sitting out in the middle of nowhere," Jobie said. "We hauled it back to camp and Kiram has it in this shack he built."

Walt pushed through a tangle of tree branches and vines and emerged in a small clearing, no larger than the average living room. A wall of green surrounded it, with a circle of blue sky high overhead. No shot-up car or skeleton occupied the space, but a different kind of oddity that sent a cold chill up Walt's spine.

"Is that a grave?" he asked, pointing to the mound of disturbed earth, a makeshift cross at its head.

Chapter Eight

"The Prophet is not going to like this." Jobie shook his head as the three men stared at the grave in the middle of the clearing.

Walt studied the area around the burial site. There were no clear footprints, and the soil had settled some, though he couldn't tell if the grave had been dug in the past few days or the past few weeks. No plants grew on the surface of the mound, and the wood on the cross was new enough the cut edges were still fresh. "We need to notify the Rangers," Walt said. "They'll want to investigate."

"Cell phones don't work out here," Jobie said. "So none of us have them."

"We'll have to talk to the Prophet," Slate said. "It's up to him."

Walt started to point out that the grave was on public land and it wasn't up to Daniel Metwater to decide whether or not it should be reported, but he didn't waste his breath. "Come on," he said. "Let's get back to camp."

They gathered up the firewood they had collected and Walt led the way back toward camp. Kiram met them at the edge of the clearing. "What took you so long?" he asked.

"We have to talk to the Prophet," Slate said.

"He doesn't like to be disturbed before dinner," Kiram said.

"He's going to want to know about what we found while we were looking for wood," Jobie said.

"What did you find?" Kiram asked.

"We'll tell the Prophet," Walt said. He pushed past the bearded man, dropped his load of wood beside the fire ring then strode toward Metwater's RV. Jobie and Slate hurried to catch up with him, Kiram following, his face like a thundercloud.

Metwater opened the door before Walt could even knock. "Is something wrong?" he asked, letting his gaze drift over the four men who gathered on the steps of the RV.

Jobie, Slate and Kiram all looked at Walt. "We found a grave while we were looking for firewood," he said. "It looks pretty fresh."

"Whose grave?" Metwater asked.

"The marker didn't say," Jobie said—as if this was a perfectly reasonable question.

"We need to notify the Rangers," Walt said. "They can determine who's in the grave."

"Maybe it's that girl the cops were looking for," Jobie said.

"If the grave is hers, I'm sure the police will find it before long," Metwater said. "We should stay out of this."

"It's too late for that," Walt said. "We found it and now we have to report it."

Metwater put his hand on Walt's shoulder and looked into his eyes, his expression that of a father dealing with an unruly—and perhaps stupid—child. "You aren't a part of that outside world anymore," he said. "Here in the Family we don't concern ourselves with the world's evil. That is for others, not us."

"You can't divorce yourself from responsibilities that way," Walt said.

"That's exactly what we're doing, living here in the wilderness," Metwater said.

"Wilderness supported by taxpayer money. You're happy enough to take advantage of that."

Metwater shook his head. "You have a long way to go toward gaining the understanding necessary to be a true member of the Family," he said. "Your wife is much more in tune with our purpose than you are."

"And you know that from talking with her for what, twenty minutes?"

"Women are much more intuitive about these things than most men. It's one of the reasons they are so drawn to my teachings."

And it has nothing to do with naked muscles and flowing hair, Walt thought cynically. "You can't let that grave go unreported," he said.

"That's exactly what we will do," Metwater said. "Although I will meditate on the problem and if I receive different guidance I will act on it." He clapped a hand on Walt's shoulder. "Come. We are having a special meal to welcome you and Serenity to the fold."

"Her name is Hannah," Walt said, reluctantly falling into step beside Metwater, since the alternative seemed to be wrestling with the man, which probably wouldn't go over well with Kiram and the others.

"But you and she are starting a new life here. Serenity suits her. She strikes me as someone who is looking for peace in her life."

Hannah was looking for her missing niece—but maybe Metwater wasn't so far off track. Maybe having the baby in her life would bring Hannah more peace of mind, and ease some of her grief for her sister. Walt wanted to help her find the baby, and the closure adopting her niece might bring.

In order to do that, he had to walk a fine line between doing anything that might blow his cover or anger Metwater to the point where he threw them out of camp, and continuing to uphold his duty as a law officer.

They reached the camp's outdoor kitchen, where most of the residents were already lined up awaiting the meal. Jobie and Slate took their places in line, while Kiram hovered near Metwater. Was he some sort of bodyguard, or simply awaiting more orders from the Prophet?

Kiram looked over and caught Walt watching him. Certainly there was little peace and love in his eyes. Walt spotted Hannah and started toward her, but Kiram grabbed his arm. "Don't get any ideas about sneaking out of camp to go to the police," he said, keeping his voice low. "Try it and you will be punished."

"I'm trembling in my boots," Walt said.

"You should be." He gave Walt's arm a shake, then released his hold. "And remember—you won't be the only one hurt." He turned to Hannah, and the icy hatred in his eyes chilled Walt to the bone.

"WHAT'S WRONG WITH YOU?" Hannah asked when she finally cornered Walt at their tent after supper that evening. They hadn't been able to exchange more than a few words during the day, constantly surrounded as they were by Family members who were either eager to welcome them, curious to know more about them or both. After breakfast, they had both been assigned to work teams to clean up, and after that had been a speech—or more like a sermon—from Metwater. Though Hannah could admit he was a charismatic speaker, she was too focused on Walt to pay much attention to Metwater's message. He sat across from her with a group of men, scowling at the Prophet as if the man had just kicked his dog.

The afternoon was taken up by more work. Hannah stayed with the women and did her best to avoid

Metwater. She spent most of her time with Phoenix, taking every opportunity to hold the baby, growing more and more sure that this was her sister's child. She was relieved to finally have the chance to be alone with Walt again after supper, to tell him all she had learned.

"I have to find a way to sneak out of here for a few hours tonight without anyone noticing," he said.

The thought of him leaving her alone here sent a spike of panic through her. "Why do you have to leave?" she asked.

He glanced around. "Let's not talk out here." He unzipped the tent flap. "Inside. And keep your voice down."

She crawled into the tent ahead of him and sat cross-legged on one of the sleeping bags he had unrolled. He moved in after her, zipping up the tent behind him. "Why do you need to leave?" she asked, her voice just above a whisper.

"When I was out gathering firewood this morning with two other men, we found a grave."

"A grave? A *person's* grave?" Her voice rose on the last word and he gripped her hand.

"Keep your voice down," he said.

She nodded, then, realizing he probably couldn't see her, said, "Okay, but what are you talking about? You found someone buried out here in the middle of nowhere?"

"I don't know what's in the grave, but I need to get word to the Rangers so they can investigate."

"You don't think it was from some pioneer ranching family or something?" she asked. "I mean, wasn't some of the parkland private land at one time?"

"This wasn't like that," he said. "I'm pretty sure it was more recent. Much more recent."

A chilling thought struck her and she gripped his hand more tightly. "That girl the Rangers are looking for?"

"I don't know," Walt said. "It's a possibility."

"The women I was working with this morning said she was here—in camp," she said. "But that she left after less than a day. Metwater supposedly sent her away because she was too young."

"I'll be sure and let the Rangers know when I talk to them. If Metwater and his followers are lying about not knowing her, I have to wonder what else they're covering up."

"The men you were with—do they know about this grave?"

"Yes. They saw it, too. Two men, Jobie and Slate. We told Metwater when we got back to camp and he refused to go to the police, or to let us go."

"He can't keep you from telling them," she said. "We came here voluntarily. He can't make us stay."

"He thinks he can."

Something in his words ratcheted her fear up another notch. "Did he threaten you?"

"He didn't, but a man named Kiram did. He's the guy I told you about—Metwater's enforcer. He said if I tried to leave, I would be punished." He took her other hand. "He said you would be, too. In fact, instead of me leaving and coming back, I'm beginning to think we should leave together and not come back. Maybe this undercover op was a bad idea."

"No, we can't leave." She pulled her hands from his. "Not when we're so close to finding Joy and learning what happened to Emily. In fact, I think I've already found Joy."

"What? Where?" He shifted toward her.

She took a deep breath, trying to organize her thoughts, but all that brought her was his scent, distracting and sensual. Heat curled through her, and the space inside the tent suddenly seemed too intimate. If she leaned over just a little, they would be touching, and her skin tingled in anticipation…

"Do you think one of the children in camp is your niece?" Walt prompted.

"Yes. The woman who came to get me to help with breakfast this morning—Phoenix—is a little older than some of the rest of the women here, maybe in her early forties. She has a fourteen-year-old daughter, Sophie. But she also has a baby. A little girl, about four months old."

"Why do you think this baby is Joy?"

"Phoenix isn't breast-feeding her. She's using formula. She told me she wasn't able to breast-feed, but I think she's lying."

"Lots of women use formula. It doesn't mean the baby isn't hers."

"No, but I held this baby. I looked into her eyes. They were Emily's eyes. The same shape—the same color." She wished she could see his face more clearly, to judge if he believed her, but the light was too dim to make out his features.

"What color are Phoenix's eyes?" he asked.

The question caught her off guard. She tried to bring Phoenix to mind, to remember her eyes, but she couldn't. "I don't know," she admitted.

He took her hand again, gentle this time. His voice was gentle, too, when he spoke. "I know you want to find your niece, and that you have good reason to believe she's with Metwater. But you can't let your natural biases lead you into a mistake. Think about how much pain it would cause Phoenix if this baby really is hers, and not Joy?"

She wanted to insist that she knew this baby was Emily's daughter, but the part of her that relied on logic instead of emotion told her that everything he said made perfect sense. "Then we have to stay here and look for proof," she said. "If I make friends with Phoenix, and with Sophie, maybe I can persuade them to tell me the truth about the baby."

"I still have to let the Rangers know about the grave we found."

"Of course." She slid her hand from his and clenched it in her lap. "I'll be fine. After all, it's nighttime. Everyone will be sleeping."

"Stay in the tent. I should be back before morning." He moved toward the door.

"Let me come with you to the bike," she said. "I can serve as a lookout until you get safely away." And she wanted to prolong the time before he left her alone.

"All right. We'd better go now. The sooner I can get away, the sooner I'll be back."

They crept through the darkened camp, keeping to the edges, skirting any lights that still shone outside tents or trailers. Walt held Hannah's hand, and she took comfort from his strong grip pulling her along, his sure steps guiding hers as they moved through the darkness.

They found the bike where they had left it, on the edge of the parking area. Walt had cut tree branches and draped them over the motorcycle to hide it from curious eyes. He quickly pulled these away and pushed the bike toward the road. "I won't start it until I'm farther from camp," he said. "If anyone comes to the tent looking for me, tell them I'm asleep."

"I will."

"And take this." He pressed something hard into her hand.

She looked down at a knife—similar to the one she had used to peel potatoes this morning. "I palmed it at dinner," he said. "It's not much, but I didn't feel right leaving you defenseless. You can keep it in your pocket."

"All right." She slipped the knife into the pocket of her skirt, where it rested, heavy and awkward, a reminder of the danger they might be in here, but an even stronger reminder that Walt was looking out for her, even when he couldn't be with her. The knowledge shook her—she had spent so many years alone. She was used to looking after herself, so what did it mean that knowing he was on her side felt so good? She looked toward the road, a faint pale strip in the light of a quarter moon. It would take Walt more than an hour to reach a good phone signal he could use to report his find—an hour traveling over rough, narrow roads in pitch-blackness. An unseen pothole, an animal running out in front of him—or one of Metwater's men in pursuit—and he might never reach his destination at all.

"Be careful." She took hold of his arm and leaned toward him, intending only to kiss his cheek. But he turned toward her and their lips met, and she realized this was what she had wanted all along—what she had wanted in that dark, intimate interlude in the tent. He brought one hand up to caress her cheek and she angled her mouth under his. He kissed the same way he did everything—with a quiet strength that moved her more than Metwater's overt seduction ever could. The brush of his unshaven cheeks abrading her skin sent a shiver of arousal through her, and she leaned in closer, wanting to be nearer to him, wanting this moment to never end.

But at last he pulled away, though his hand remained on her shoulder, steadying her. "I'll be back as soon as I can," he said. "Stay safe."

"You, too." Reluctantly, she stepped back, one hand to her mouth as if to preserve the memory of his kiss. She watched him as he walked away, pushing the motorcycle, until he was out of sight, disappearing into the darkness. Then she crossed the bridge back into camp.

She retraced the route they had followed back to the tent, seeing and hearing no one. The few lanterns that had previously been lit were out now, plunging the compound into silent blackness. Hannah felt her way from tree to tree, wishing she had thought to bring a flashlight with her. She let out a sigh of relief when she spotted the tent, by itself on the edge of the camp.

She had almost reached the safety of that shelter when someone clamped a hand over her mouth and dragged her back against him. She kicked out and tried to struggle free, but the unseen man held her fast. "Where is your husband now?" a voice growled in her ear. "And why isn't he here to protect you?"

Chapter Nine

Walt estimated he had walked the heavy motorcycle the better part of a mile before he dared climb on and start the engine. It roared to life, echoing in the midnight stillness. If anyone in camp heard him and figured out what was going on, he would be long gone before they could come after him.

He raced the bike as fast as he dared over the rough washboard road, barely maintaining control of the big machine as it bounced over the rugged dirt track. His headlight seemed to scarcely penetrate the inky blackness, illuminating only a few yards in front of him. More than once eyes glowed from the brush alongside the road—coyotes or foxes or other wild creatures observing his passing.

He tried not to think of what might happen to Hannah while he was away. Instead, he focused on the memory of that goodbye kiss. Working with her on this undercover op, he had grown close to her in a very short period of time. Even though they weren't married, at times he felt that close connection to her—or at least, what he hoped the connection between a husband and wife should feel like.

The kind of connection he had wanted with his former girlfriend, but had clearly never had. Looking back, he remembered how stunned he had been when he learned she was seeing his brother. But he saw, too, how part of him wasn't surprised she had betrayed him. Wanting someone to love you deeply wasn't the same as having that love be a reality. It was a lesson he had had to learn the hard way.

So why was he even thinking about love and Hannah in the same breath? As beautiful as she was, and as close as he felt to her at times, she was here to find her niece. She wanted to return to her home in Texas and start a new life with the baby—nowhere in that plan did he see room for a backcountry cop. He was doing it again—wishing for a relationship that couldn't exist.

It was almost two in the morning when he finally reached the paved highway that led toward Black Canyon of the Gunnison National Park and Ranger Brigade headquarters. He raced the bike over the blacktop to the headquarters building and let himself in with his key, then dialed the commander's number on the office line, more reliable than cell service out here.

Ranger Brigade commander Graham Ellison didn't sound groggy when he answered the phone. "Ellison. What's up?"

"It's Walt Riley, sir. There's been a development near Metwater's compound that you need to be aware of." He explained about the grave and its approximate location, as well as Metwater's stricture against reporting it. "I took a chance, sneaking out of camp," Walt said. "I need to get back as soon as possible."

"Wait there at headquarters. I'll have someone there in half an hour or less. We need you to show us the area on a map and fill in some details."

"Yes, sir." He hung up the phone and settled in to wait.

KIRAM WRENCHED HANNAH'S arm behind her back, hurting her. "I'm going to uncover your mouth," he said. "But if you cry out, I'll break your arm."

She nodded to show she understood and he removed his hand. "Let me go," she said.

"Where is your husband?" he asked.

"He's asleep in the tent."

"I was just there. He isn't there."

"Maybe he got up to go to the bathroom." She began to struggle again, frantic over what he might do to her if she didn't get away. He started pulling her toward the parking lot—toward the deserted road and the empty wilderness, away from the rest of the camp, where there were people who might help her. "What are you doing?" she asked. "Where are you taking me?"

"I warned your husband what would happen if he disobeyed the Prophet's orders."

"I don't know what you're talking about. Let me go. Help!"

The savage jerk he gave her didn't break her arm, but it hurt enough that she gasped in pain. "You're making a mistake," she said. "Let's go to the Prophet now. I'll prove to you that you're making a mistake." She had no idea what she would say to Metwater, but demanding to see him would at least get her back to the camp, where surely someone would help her.

Kiram stopped. "You want to see the Prophet?"

"Yes. He's the leader of this camp. If he thinks I need to be punished, I want to hear it from him."

"Fine. We'll go to him." He turned and headed back toward camp, still gripping her arm. She had to run to keep from being dragged. The clearing in the midst of the tents and trailers was empty and silent, the only light from the dying coals of the bonfire they had gathered around earlier. Metwater's motor home was dark and silent also.

Hannah slowed her steps as they neared the RV. "The Prophet won't like being awakened," she said.

"You should have thought of that before your husband disobeyed him." One hand gripping her arm, he raised the other hand to knock on the door of the motor home.

Hannah didn't wait for someone to answer Kiram's knock. She had no intention of going into that

RV with him—not in the middle of the night, with no witnesses around to notice if the two men decided to make her disappear altogether. She slipped her hand into the pocket of her skirt and gripped the knife Walt had given her. As her fingers closed around the blade, she summoned all her courage. She was doing this for Joy, she told herself. For Emily.

She jabbed the knife hard into Kiram's shoulder. He yelped and released her, and she ran to the far side of the dying bonfire. Snatching a smoldering branch from the fire, she brandished it in one hand, the knife in the other. Then she began to scream. "Help! Some-one help me, please! Kiram attacked me! Help!"

As she had hoped, heads poked out of the tents and trailers surrounding the area. Kiram clutched his shoulder, blood trickling between his fingers. "She stabbed me!" he roared, and started toward her, his face a mask of rage.

"Only because he attacked me first. Look at the bruises on my arm if you don't believe me."

No one moved to help her, but none of them went back inside, either. Kiram glared at her. The light out-side the motor home went on and the door opened to reveal Daniel Metwater, clad only in pajama pants, scowling at them. "What is going on?" he asked.

"The new man, Walt, left tonight," Kiram said. "I'm sure he went to the police."

"Of course he went to the police," Hannah said. "There's a fresh grave out there, not far from camp, and the police are looking for a missing woman. Her family is probably beside themselves, trying to find her."

"We don't have anything to do with that," Metwater said.

"Trying to hide it makes you look like you do." Hannah slipped the knife into her pocket but kept hold of the smoldering branch. "And the fact that Walt went to tell someone about the grave doesn't give Kiram any right to attack me."

Metwater turned to Kiram. "Did you attack her?"

"I warned her husband if he disobeyed your orders and left the camp, they would have to be disciplined." He lifted his hand from his shoulder. "And she stabbed me."

"When a man puts his hands on a woman against her will, she has a right to defend herself," Hannah said.

Murmurs of agreement rose from the crowd of onlookers. Metwater held up a hand. "Part of being a member of the Family is agreeing to abide by my rules," he said.

"One of your rules is that women are to be treated with respect."

Hannah turned to see who had spoken. Phoenix stepped into the circle of light from a lantern that hung outside her tent. She cradled the baby in her arms. "If Kiram attacked Serenity in the darkness, when her husband wasn't there to defend her, that isn't treating her with respect."

"What about respect for me and my role of carrying out the Prophet's will?" Kiram growled the words. At that moment, he reminded Hannah of a wounded bear.

Everyone was focused on Metwater, as if he really was some king or Old Testament prophet who had authority to rule their lives. Hannah realized she was holding her breath in anticipation, as if she believed he had power over her, as well. Had Emily stood before him like this, waiting while he decided her fate?

Of course, all she had to do was declare she had had enough of this nonsense and walk away. But doing so would end her best chance of finding out what had happened to Emily and her baby. She shifted her gaze to where Phoenix stood, cradling the child. That baby might be Joy. Hannah couldn't walk away until she knew for sure.

"Tomorrow, after Serenity's husband has returned, we will hold a council," Metwater declared. "At that time, we will decide the appropriate response to their willful and disobedient behavior." He fixed his gaze on Hannah. A shiver crept up her spine. Did no one else see the malevolence in those dark eyes? "Until tomorrow, I put you in Phoenix's care. She will watch over you."

"I don't need a guard," Hannah said.

Metwater's smile held no warmth. "But clearly, you do."

Phoenix crossed the clearing to Hannah's side. "Come on," she said. "I'll fix a comfortable place for you in my trailer." She leaned closer, her voice so soft Hannah scarcely heard her words, and she was sure no one else could. "You'll be safer with me than alone in your tent—just in case Kiram gets any ideas."

Hannah glanced at Kiram, who was still glowering at her. Her aching arm reminded her of how easily he could overpower her. She nodded. "Thanks," she said. She wouldn't think of this time as imprisonment. She would use the opportunity to get to know Phoenix and her baby better. Maybe this would be the key to learning the truth she needed to know.

MEMBERS OF THE Ranger team started showing up at headquarters within half an hour of Walt's call—Lance Carpenter arrived first, followed by Michael Dance, Ethan Reynolds and the commander. Walt had made coffee and they helped themselves to mugs before settling down to consider the case. "Sorry for almost blowing your cover out there yesterday," Lance said as he settled at the conference table across from Walt. "We should have checked in with the commander before we headed out there."

"It worked out okay," Walt said. "Now Metwater and the rest think I'm as disgruntled with the cops as they are."

"Tell us more about this grave you found," Commander Ellison said, settling into the chair at the head of the table.

"It looks fairly recent, though I'm no expert," Walt said. "It was in a small clearing, not visible until you were right up on it, about a mile from camp, at least that far from any road."

"And you're sure it was a grave?" Michael asked.

"It was an oblong mound of earth, maybe two feet wide and four feet long, with a homemade wooden cross at one end. No writing on the cross. No footprints on the surrounding ground. The dirt had dried out and settled a little, but no vegetation was growing on it, and the sawed ends of the cross were fresh, not weathered." He sat back in his chair. "And Metwater was very annoyed when I told him I intended to report it."

"What was his argument against doing so?" Ethan asked.

"It would bring law enforcement into camp again."

"What is he afraid we're going to find?" Lance asked. "He sounds like a man with something to hide."

"Do you think he knows anything about the missing woman—Lucia Raton?" Graham asked.

"Hannah spoke to some Family members who said she came around wanting to join the group," Walt said. "Metwater supposedly sent her away because she was too young."

"And they didn't bother to mention this to us," Michael said. "I think this warrants questioning him again. Maybe we should bring him in."

"Let's see what we find in the grave first." Graham sat back in his chair. "We'll get a team out there at first light, though we'll have to wait for a forensic anthropologist to excavate it properly. That could take a while, depending on where he or she has to come from. If it's Denver or Salt Lake, it could mean an extra day's wait."

"You should at least get someone out there to guard the site," Walt said. "Now that Metwater knows I know about this, if he is involved somehow, he may try to destroy evidence."

"We'll do that," Graham said. "What else have you learned?"

"Metwater preaches a message of peace and love, but he's set a lot of rules for his followers. He's got at least one guy, calls himself Kiram, whose job is to enforce the rules. He threatened me—and Hannah—if I came to you."

"Threatened you with what?" Lance asked.

"Nothing specific. I told Hannah I'd feel better if she came with me tonight," Walt said. "I gave her the opportunity to call off the operation altogether, but she wanted to stay and see it through."

"Any news about her sister or the baby?" Ethan asked.

"Everyone denies knowing anything about the sister, but I think they're lying," Walt said. "There's a woman in camp who has a little girl the right age to be Hannah's niece, but we don't have any proof she isn't the woman's child. Hannah thinks if she makes friends with the woman, who goes by Phoenix, she can find out more."

"We'll give it another day or two, but if either of you feel at any time that you're in danger, get out of there," Graham said. "If this bunch really is responsible for Lucia Raton's death, we don't want to give them a chance to add to the body count."

"When I described Hannah's sister to some men in the camp, one of them told me she sounded like a woman who was there in the spring," Walt said. "Hannah said Metwater reacted to the name, though he denied knowing Emily."

"Before I forget, we managed to get hold of Marsha Caldwell." Marco leaned back to snag a notebook off a desk. "The nurse who witnessed Emily Dietrich's will."

"What did she say?" Walt asked, tensed on the edge of his chair.

"She remembered Emily—described her as a sweet young woman with a beautiful baby. Caldwell said Emily didn't strike her as particularly fearful. She came to the hospital with another woman—the Anna Ingels who also witnessed the will. She thought Ingels was a friend or maybe an older relative."

"Did you get a description of Ingels?" Walt asked.

Marco consulted his notes. "Nothing really useful. Medium height, late thirties, blond hair and light eyes."

That description could fit a few of the women in camp, but it wasn't specific enough to zero in on anyone. "How could she say Emily wasn't fearful when she wanted Caldwell to witness a will?"

"She said it wasn't the first will she had witnessed," Marco said. "Apparently, labor and delivery is traumatic for some women. She said it makes them aware of their own mortality. Add in the responsibility for a new life, and a will outlining who should care for the baby in the event of the mother's death is a sensible response."

"So she didn't think Emily was afraid someone was going to kill her?" Walt asked.

"She didn't think so, no."

Was Hannah wrong, then? Had her sister died of an unfortunate bout of ill health, and Metwater had nothing to do with it? So why was he trying to hide the child—assuming Phoenix's baby really was Hannah's niece, as she asserted? He shoved back his chair. "I had better get back to camp," he said. "Even though I don't think Kiram would be foolish enough to try anything, I don't like leaving Hannah there too long."

"You may be in the best position to learn what happened with Lucia Raton," Michael said. "Whatever evidence you can find could be crucial to making a case."

Walt nodded. As long as Metwater and his people saw Walt and Hannah as prospective members who were interested in the Prophet's teachings, they were more likely to let down their guard and reveal information that could help solve one or more crimes. Provided Walt could hold on to his cover long enough and get back in Metwater's good graces after disobeying orders and coming here tonight. He was going to have to do some fast talking to do so, but maybe Metwater's desire to keep Hannah around would work in their favor. "I'll try to learn as much as I can," he said.

Graham walked with him to the door and shook his hand. "We'll be back in camp after we've searched the grave. We'll let you know what we find then."

"By that time, I hope Hannah and I are ready to leave. Everything in camp looks innocent enough, but something about the whole setup rubs me the wrong way. Metwater is up to something—we just haven't figured out what yet."

Chapter Ten

Hannah spent a restless night on a sofa on one side of the travel trailer Phoenix shared with her daughter Sophie and the baby. Worries over where Walt might be and what he might be doing competed with nightmares of Kiram or Daniel Metwater leering over her to prevent sleep. Had Walt made it safely to the road? What would the Rangers do with the information he gave them? Was the grave that of the missing young woman? Who had killed her and put her there? Had Kiram merely been trying to frighten her when he had grabbed her earlier, or had he really intended to hurt her? Had Emily suffered a similar fright, which had eventually led to her death?

She tried to distract herself by focusing on the baby. Little Vicki slept in a porta-crib next to Phoenix's bed, and Hannah could just see her from the sofa. The child slept peacefully, fist in her mouth, clad in a pink fleece sleeper. Hannah fought the urge to take the baby from the crib and cuddle her. But that would only awaken Phoenix and the baby and arouse suspicion. And it wouldn't really tell Hannah anything, only satisfy her longing to hold the child in her arms.

Phoenix awakened at dawn to tend to the baby. Hannah sat up on the sofa, a blanket wrapped around her, and watched as the older woman prepared a bottle of formula. "Would you like to feed her while I get dressed?" Phoenix asked.

"Yes." Hannah held out her arms and took the child, who stared up at her with sleepy eyes. Vicki took the bottle readily and Hannah settled back to marvel at the baby's sweet perfection. Sophie got out of her bunk and came to sit beside her.

"She eats like a little piglet," the girl said, letting the baby latch on to her index finger.

"She's always had a healthy appetite." Phoenix emerged from her bedroom and joined them. "I'm grateful for that."

"Would you think I was terribly nosy if I asked about her father?" Hannah kept her eyes focused on the baby, though she braced herself for Phoenix's answer.

"The Prophet is her father," Phoenix said, unflustered by the question.

"Oh. I didn't know."

Phoenix removed the now-empty bottle from Vicki's mouth. "I'll take her now," she said, and raised the baby to her shoulder and began patting her back.

"He's the father to all the children here," Phoenix said. "If not physically, then certainly spiritually."

Sophie made a face. "He's not my father," she said.

"Now, Sophie," her mother said.

Sophie turned to Hannah. "My father is a musician in San Francisco. But we don't see him much." She shrugged. "It's okay. He's kind of messed up."

"Sophie, why don't you run ahead to help Starfall and the others with breakfast," Phoenix said. "Serenity and I will be along soon."

"She doesn't like it when I talk about my dad," Sophie said, standing. "She and the Prophet are big into forgetting the past, but I don't see how anyone can really do that, do you?"

"Sophie!"

"I'm going." Grinning, the girl skipped from the trailer.

Phoenix settled onto the sofa beside Hannah. "I'm sorry about that," she said. "I guess Sophie is a little young to understand all the spiritual concepts the Prophet is trying to teach us."

"You mean, about forgetting the past."

"Maybe not forgetting." She laid the baby across her lap and began removing her diaper. "But putting it behind us. She and I made a fresh start when we came here. It's time to look forward, not backward." Her eyes met Hannah's. "We all have things in our past we would like to not dwell on."

"Yes. But the past shapes us," Hannah said. "We are who we are because of it."

"I would rather not remember the pain," Phoenix said. "I want to focus on the future." She fastened the baby's diaper and smiled down at the child. "Let's go to breakfast," she said.

"The Prophet said last night you were in charge of me," Hannah said as they made their way through camp toward the outdoor kitchen. "Does that mean you're my guard? Will you get in trouble if I leave?"

"Think of me as your companion." She hooked her arm in Hannah's. "I'm watching out for you and helping you. There's no need for you to be alone."

"My husband will be back soon," she said, resisting the urge to pull away from the other woman.

"He'll be assigned a companion, as well. The two of you will be kept apart until the council."

Hannah stopped. "Why?"

"It's for your own good," Phoenix said. "So that you can think more clearly, and so that you will be fairly judged separately and not as a single unit. His crimes don't have to reflect on you."

"Walt hasn't committed any crime," Hannah said. "He did the right thing, notifying the police about that grave."

Phoenix's gaze shifted away, and her mouth grew pinched. "Disobeying the Prophet is wrong," she said. "He has good reasons for all of his decisions. If you want to be a part of the Family, you need to realize that." She took Hannah's hand. "Come on. We'll be late for breakfast. You'll feel better after you eat."

Hannah tugged her hand free, but walked beside Phoenix to the cook tent. She left her with the other women and got in line for oatmeal and dried berries, then found a seat on a bench next to Sophie. "Did you and Mom have a fight about something?" Sophie asked.

"Your mother thinks my husband should be punished because he disobeyed the Prophet, even though he was doing the right thing," Hannah said.

"It's a big deal to disobey the Prophet," Sophie said. "It almost never happens."

"Who was the last person to break one of his rules?" Hannah asked.

Sophie dug into her bowl of oatmeal. "We're not supposed to talk about it."

"I didn't know the person, so what could it hurt?" Hannah said. "Maybe by telling me who they were and what they did, you could help me not to make the same mistake."

Sophie considered this. "It was a girl called Freedom. Well, that's what the Prophet called her. I don't think it was her real name."

"What did she do that was so wrong?" Hannah asked.

"She wanted to run away."

Hannah set aside her own spoon, a cold hollow in

the pit of her stomach. “I thought anyone was free to leave here whenever he or she chose.”

“Most people are. But Freedom had a baby, and all children belong to the Prophet. So she could have left, but she would have had to leave her baby behind.”

“No mother would do that,” Hannah said.

Sophie shrugged. “I guess she wanted to leave badly enough that she did.”

Hannah stared at the girl for a moment, letting this information sink in. “You mean, she left the Family, and didn’t take her baby with her?”

Sophie ducked her head. “I shouldn’t have said anything. Please don’t tell Mom. I’ll get in trouble.”

“I won’t tell her, I promise.” Hannah covered the child’s hand with her own and lowered her voice to a whisper. “That’s why you have Vicki, isn’t it?” she asked. “She was Freedom’s baby.”

Sophie nodded. “Please don’t tell.”

Hannah squeezed her hand. “I won’t. I promise.” Freedom must have been Emily. Vicki—Victory—was Joy. And she belonged to Hannah now. Not Phoenix or the Prophet or anyone else.

WALT HALF EXPECTED to be met in the parking area outside the camp by Kiram and a crowd of angry Family members, but the lot was vacant, only the chattering of a scolding squirrel greeting him. He parked the bike, covered it with the branches he had cut earlier and crossed the bridge into camp. Jobie met him at the other side, a staff in one hand, a breakfast burrito in the other. "Hey," he said by way of greeting. "You missed all the excitement with your wife and Kiram last night."

Walt froze, one hand automatically reaching for the service weapon that wasn't at his side. "What happened with Hannah and Kiram?" he asked, his mind racing. If that thug had hurt Hannah…

"She says he was manhandling her and she called him on it and made a big fuss in front of the Prophet and everyone." He took a bite of his breakfast and chewed.

"Was he hurting her?" Walt asked. "And why?"

"He said she needed to be punished because the two of you were disobeying the Prophet's orders." He shrugged. "One of his jobs is to keep people in line, but he has a rep for taking things too far. A couple of other women have complained, but I guess the Prophet has let him get away with it until now. No way he could ignore the stink your wife was making last night, though."

Good for Hannah, Walt thought. "What did the Prophet do?"

"He sent Serenity off to stay with Phoenix and told Kiram to leave her alone. There's going to be a special council tonight to decide what your punishment should be for breaking the rules and leaving camp to go to the police."

Let them try to lay a hand on him or Hannah and

see how far they got. Walt started to push past Jobie. "Her name isn't Serenity, it's Hannah, and I need to see her."

Jobie tried to block him and Walt raised his fist, as if to take a swing. Jobie took a step back. "Hey, chill, dude! I was just going to tell you it's a good idea to play it cool. Kiram is still really ticked about being called out in front of the whole camp, so it would be smart to steer clear of him until tonight."

What he wanted was to confront Kiram right now and maybe pound his face for laying a hand on Hannah, but doing so would be letting emotion take the lead instead of using common sense. "What happens at these council meetings?" he asked.

"The Prophet usually gives a talk, then each side gets to present their case, then the Prophet makes a ruling." He shrugged. "He'll probably just have everyone involved do some kind of community service like pick up trash or build a new shelter. It's no big deal."

"Where is Hannah now?"

"She's eating breakfast with Phoenix and Sophie. She's fine."

"I still want to see her." He started forward once more and this time Jobie stepped aside to let him pass.

Conversation stopped abruptly when Walt walked into the open-sided shed that served as the Family's dining hall. Kiram looked up from his seat at the end of one of the long wooden picnic tables and glared at Walt, but remained silent. Everyone else stared, some openmouthed with avid curiosity, others avoiding his gaze, clearly fearful. Walt spotted Hannah, sitting next to a young girl, and started toward her. She rose to meet him and, without speaking, he took her arm and led her away from the shelter.

The murmur of conversation rose again behind them. Hannah gripped his arm. "How did it go?" she asked. "Are the Rangers on their way?"

"They're sending a team out to investigate the grave, then they'll want to question Metwater and others in the camp."

"That won't go over well," she said, glancing back toward the tables. Kiram had moved from his seat and stood at the edge of the shelter, watching them.

"They need to explain why they lied about Lucia Raton having been in camp," Walt said. "And why Metwater was so insistent I not report the grave to law enforcement."

"Some of the people here feel the police are invading their privacy with all their questions."

"It's our job to invade people's privacy, if that's what it takes to solve a crime."

"I know." She patted his arm. "But I see their point, too. Not wanting the police here doesn't make them guilty of anything."

"Maybe not. But lying is almost always suspicious." He smoothed his hand down her arm and she winced. "What's wrong?" he asked, immediately tensed. "Are you hurt?"

"Just a little bruised where Kiram grabbed me." She rubbed the arm. "He caught me walking back toward our tent after you left last night."

"Jobie told me you called him out in front of a crowd and that Metwater ordered him to leave you alone."

"Yes. Kiram says he was acting on Metwater's authority, but I'm not so sure. I think he's just a bully." She glanced over her shoulder at the glowering young man. "I'm probably his least favorite person right now."

"He's my least favorite person, so that makes us even." He glared at Kiram. The man was going to be trouble, but Walt would wait to deal with him. He turned back to Hannah. "You're sure you're all right?"

"Yes." She took his arm and led him farther away from the crowd. "Better than all right," she said. "Phoenix's daughter, Sophie, admitted this morning that the baby isn't her mother's. She belonged to a Family member who called herself Freedom. I'm sure she means Emily."

"How did Phoenix end up with the baby?"

"Sophie said the mother, Freedom, wanted to run away. The Prophet said she could leave, but she would have to leave her baby behind, because all children belong to him or some such nonsense." She frowned. "Phoenix told me Metwater was the baby's father, but I know that isn't right. But apparently, he claims to be the father of all the children in the camp, whether he actually is or not."

"So what happened when he told her she could leave but he would keep her baby?" Walt asked.

"Sophie said Freedom left anyway, and Phoenix was given the baby to care for. But I know Emily wouldn't have left the baby behind. Not voluntarily."

"It sounds as if Sophie doesn't know Emily—if Freedom really is Emily—is dead," Walt said. "Maybe she wasn't told because she's still a child."

"Or maybe no one was told because Metwater didn't want anyone to know about his involvement in her death. Emily died in Denver, when the Family was already living here on park land. It would have been easy enough to bring the baby back from Denver after Emily died and tell everyone the mother had abandoned her."

"Maybe Emily left, intending to come back, and died before she could," he said.

"Emily would never have abandoned her baby. Never." Hannah's voice shook and she sounded on the verge of tears.

Walt took her by the shoulders. "It's okay," he said. "Keep talking with Phoenix and Sophie and see what else you can learn. There's still a chance the baby belongs to some other woman and not your sister."

"Vicki is Emily's baby, I know it." She clutched his arm. "Why can't we just take the baby and leave now? The DNA tests will prove I'm right."

"We need to stay as long as we can and learn as much as we can," he said. "We may never have a better opportunity to find out not just what happened to your sister, but to Lucia Raton."

She looked stubborn and Walt braced himself for her arguments. He was prepared to tell her that she could leave with the investigative team when they showed up to question Family members about Lucia, but that he needed to stay behind to gather more information. While Hannah had a court order granting her temporary custody of her sister's child, they needed a positive identification of the baby before Hannah could take her. And as long as Daniel Metwater claimed to be the child's father, and his name was on the birth certificate, he could fight Hannah in court to regain custody of the baby.

Hannah changed the subject. "There's supposed to be some kind of meeting this evening to decide our fate," she said. "I'm guessing after the cops descend on camp, everyone will vote to throw us out."

"They might," he said. "We'll have to work hard to persuade them that we're sincere."

"Do you really think the grave you found belongs to that poor girl?"

"I don't know. We'll have to wait and see."

"I've never been very good at waiting," she said. "I've always been the type to make a decision quickly and follow through." She stared at the ground between their feet. "That hasn't always worked out well for me."

"I'm more deliberate, but that doesn't mean the decisions I've made have always been the right ones," he said.

"Serenity!"

They looked up to see Phoenix hurrying toward them, a worried expression on her face. "Is something wrong?" Hannah asked. "Is Vicki okay?"

"We're fine." She stopped in front of them, a little out of breath. Up close, Walt noted the fine lines at the corners of her eyes and the deep furrow between her eyes. Hannah was right—Phoenix did look closer to forty than thirty—older than the majority of Metwater's followers. How had she ended up with the group?

"You need to come with me now," Phoenix said to Hannah. "I'm supposed to watch over you until the meeting tonight."

"Surely the Prophet won't be upset about me talking with my husband," Hannah said.

"Sometimes when two people talk together a lot, away from the group, it can look like they're plotting," Phoenix said. "It sets a bad example."

"Is that one of the lessons the Prophet teaches?" Walt asked.

Phoenix glanced at him. "The Prophet teaches many lessons," she said. "Some of them have saved my life." She took Hannah's hand and laced her fingers with the younger woman's. "Let's go. You said before you enjoy working with children. You can help me with that job this morning."

She started to lead Hannah away. "What about me?" Walt called. "What am I supposed to do until the council this evening?"

Phoenix looked over her shoulder at him. "Someone else has been assigned to watch over you," she said, then ducked her head and hurried away.

Walt heard heavy footsteps behind him. He tensed, prepared to defend himself if necessary. The new arrival said nothing.

"Kiram, I've got a score to settle with you," Walt said, turning around.

"If I ever catch you away from camp, believe me, we'll settle that score," Kiram said. "For now, you're to come with me."

"What if I refuse?" Walt asked.

"I'd be fine with you leaving camp right this minute," Kiram said. "But the Prophet wants to see you. He has a proposal for you—one you ought to listen to."

"The Prophet wants something from me?" Walt asked. That was a new twist. "What is it?"

"Come with me and find out. I'm hoping he wants me to take you out and beat you to a pulp, but then, I seldom get so lucky."

Chapter Eleven

"Where is Kiram taking Walt?" Hannah tried to pull away from Phoenix when she saw Kiram lead Walt away.

"Your husband will be all right." Phoenix was stronger than she looked and almost yanked Hannah off her feet. "You'll see him tonight, after the council. In the meantime, you can help me with the children. That's our job for the day."

"This isn't right," Hannah said, reluctantly falling into step beside Phoenix. "We shouldn't be separated like this."

"It's for your own good," Phoenix said. "After all, you have to think for yourself, even though you're married. And remember—whatever punishment the Prophet decides for you, it will make you a better person in the end."

"Have you ever been punished by the Prophet?" Hannah asked.

"When I first came here, yes. But I needed to learn an important lesson, and I was grateful for it later."

"What did you do that you needed to be punished for?" Hannah asked. The older woman looked so serene and devoted to Metwater. Hannah couldn't imagine she had ever done anything to displease him.

"That is all in the past and we don't talk about the past," she said. "Come, let's get the children. You'll feel better when you're with them."

Sophie was waiting with the other children, and a duffel bag filled with balls and stuffed animals and other toys. While Sophie and her mother organized the children into play groups, Hannah took charge of Vicki. She was an easygoing baby, seldom fussy, happy to be held and admired.

"You're so good with her," Phoenix said, coming to sit at the picnic table beside Hannah. "Do you have children?"

Hannah couldn't hold back the gasp that escaped her. "Wh-why would you ask that?" she stammered. "If I had children, they'd be here with me."

"Not necessarily. They might be with their father, or a grandparent. Not every child lives with her mother. Sometimes that isn't even the best thing."

Hannah clutched the baby more tightly. "No, I don't have any children." It wasn't a lie. Not really.

"Sophie lived with my parents for a while," she said, her expression calm as she watched her daughter. "I wasn't able to take care of her, so I signed over custody to them. One of the best things about coming here is that she's able to be with me again."

Were Phoenix's parents really happy that she was living in a trailer in the middle of nowhere, following a self-proclaimed prophet? Hannah wondered. Then again, maybe Phoenix's folks were in poor health, or simply tired of taking care of the child. It wasn't Hannah's place to judge. "She seems very happy here," she said.

"She doesn't like the Prophet, but I hope in time she'll understand his wisdom."

"Do you really think he's wise?" Hannah asked.

She smiled serenely. Or was her serenity merely a kind of naïveté? "The Prophet saved my life. I owe him everything. Apollo, what is that in your mouth? We don't eat bugs." She jumped up and hurried to persuade the little boy to spit out his find. Hannah cradled the baby and studied the other woman. Surely she didn't mean that Daniel Metwater had literally saved her—rescuing her from drowning or pulling her from a burning car? Following the Prophet had clearly sent Phoenix's life in another direction—away from a bad situation or wrong choices?

Phoenix returned. "How long have you and your husband been married?" she asked.

"Not long. A few months." Hannah hoped her response sounded natural. She wasn't used to lying, though she agreed that in this case, it was necessary.

"I thought about marriage a couple of times, but it never happened," Phoenix said. "Just as well, since I never stayed with any man very long." She laughed. "Good thing, or I wouldn't have met the Prophet."

"Are you and he, well, lovers?" Hadn't Phoenix hinted as much, when she said Metwater was the baby's father? Or had she said that because she believed Emily and Metwater had been a couple?

Phoenix's smile struck Hannah as a little smug. "I've enjoyed the Prophet's attentions from time to time," she said. "He tries to spend special time with each of his female followers—it's really a privilege." She patted Hannah's arm. "I'm sure your turn will come."

Hannah shuddered. She had no intention of enjoying any such "attention" from Metwater. "I doubt my husband would appreciate that."

"Oh, he'll come around in time. After all, marriage is such an outmoded concept."

Hannah recognized Metwater's words. "I think two people pledging to love each other and care for each other for the rest of their lives is timeless," she said. "An ideal that never goes out of style."

Phoenix wrinkled her nose. "But how many people actually live up to that ideal?"

"A lot whom I know," Hannah said.

"And no one I know."

Before Hannah could come up with a suitable answer, the baby began fussing. Hannah shifted and tried to comfort the infant, but her fussing soon grew to wails. “Let me take her.” Phoenix reached for the baby. “Maybe she needs changing.”

As she took the child, one sleeve of her loose peasant blouse pushed up, revealing several lines of thin, dark scars on her forearms. “What happened to your arm?” Hannah asked.

Phoenix flushed and quickly yanked the sleeve down and cradled the child. “It’s nothing. I’ll go get a fresh diaper,” she said, already heading toward the trailer. “You watch the children.”

A chill swept through Hannah, as if someone had opened a door that should have been left closed. She wished she was home, with Joy safe and the future not so uncertain. There were too many secrets in this particular family.

“I WANT TO know what you told the police.”

Daniel Metwater didn’t waste any time getting to the point when he hauled Walt in front of him. At least the Prophet was fully dressed today, in faded jeans and a white button-down with the sleeves rolled up. He sat in an upholstered chair in the living room of the RV like a man on a throne. Walt still thought he looked out of place here in the backcountry—like the kind of man who, instead of taking a five-mile hike to see the sights, would order a flunky to take the hike for him and report back.

“Why do you want to know?” Walt asked.

"Lose the attitude," Kiram said, and punched Walt in the shoulder.

Walt turned on him. "Hit me again and you'll be sorry," he said. "You can't shove me around the way you did my wife."

"Leave us, Kiram," Metwater said.

Kiram's face reddened and he worked his mouth as if trying to come up with a response. But when Metwater fixed him with a stare, the bearded man bowed his head and stormed out. Walt waited until the door closed behind him before he spoke. "Hannah has bruises on her arms where Kiram roughed her up last night," he said. "I'm not going to stand for that." He had every intention of filing assault charges against Kiram, though he hadn't discussed it with Hannah yet.

"Kiram can be a little intense in his zeal to protect the Family—and to protect me," Metwater said.

"He's a bully. If you don't rein him in, I will."

"I can take care of Kiram."

"Keep him away from me—and away from Hannah."

Metwater hesitated. Walt was sure he was going to say something about Walt needing a minder until tonight's council meeting, but after a tense few seconds, he relented. "I'll tell him to stay away."

"See that he does."

"I didn't bring you here to talk about Kiram. I want to know what you told the police."

"I told them the truth," Walt said. "That I was out looking for firewood and found what appeared to be a fairly fresh grave. They agreed it was worth checking out, especially with a young woman missing."

"No one in this camp had anything to do with that unfortunate young woman's disappearance," Metwater said.

"I've learned she was here in the camp, yet you lied when the Rangers asked if you had seen her before."

"Who told you that?" Metwater demanded.

Walt leaned against the wall that separated the RV's living area from the rest of the space, arms crossed in a deliberately casual, some might have said disrespectful, pose. "Why does it matter if it's true?" he countered.

"Because of you, officers will be disrupting our lives with their questions," Metwater said.

"No. They'll be doing that because you lied to them and tried to conceal what could be evidence of a crime. Guilty people behave that way."

"Or people who value their privacy," Metwater said.

"Sometimes it's the same thing." Walt had to force himself not to smirk. He was enjoying this too much.

"When the Rangers arrive, I want you to talk to them," Metwater said.

Walt hadn't seen this coming. "Why me?"

"Since you're the one who went to them, they'll be more likely to trust you. Tell them we had nothing to do with the grave you found or the woman who disappeared."

Walt straightened. "You tell them. I'm not your official spokesperson."

"I have more important things to do than waste time talking with the police," Metwater said.

"Such as?" Walt looked around the trailer. "Writing blog posts and preaching sermons can't take that much of your time."

Metwater stood and moved closer to Walt. They were about the same height, and had no trouble looking each other in the eye. "Why did you come here?" Metwater asked. "I don't believe it was because you want to be one of us. You have no respect for our way of life."

Sticking to his cover required Walt to lie and pretend to be a fan of Metwater and his philosophy, but after the better part of two days in camp, he didn't have the stomach for it. As long as he didn't reveal he was a law enforcement officer, sticking closer to the truth should be safe. And it might even nudge Metwater into revealing something useful. "I came here looking for a friend," he said. "She disappeared a while back and her family is worried about her."

Metwater lifted one eyebrow. "Lucia Raton is a friend of yours?"

"Not her. I'm looking for Emily Dietrich."

"Your wife's friend from school." Metwater nodded. "You think she was one of my followers?"

"She was pregnant. Her fiancé was killed and she became one of your followers. She was living with your followers the last time her sister heard from her."

"Her sister, your wife."

Walt didn't let himself react. "Why do you say that?" he asked.

"The resemblance is there."

"So you do know Emily?"

"I knew her. But she was only with us a short time."

"What about her baby?"

Metwater turned away. "I can't help you there."

"Can't—or won't?"

"You may leave now," Metwater said. "I'll see you at the council tonight."

"Tell me what happened to Emily Dietrich," Walt said.

Metwater sat and looked up at Walt, his expression calm. "I can't tell you what I don't know," he said.

Walt wanted to grab the man and shake him. But all that would probably achieve was a beating by Kiram and friends, and possible assault charges himself. "I'm going to keep asking questions," he said. "I'm going to find answers."

"I can't stop you," Metwater said. "But you might not like the answers you find. Sometimes it's wisest to let the dead rest in peace."

"What makes you say she's dead?" Walt demanded. "You do know something, don't you?"

Metwater's gaze shifted away and he waved his hand dismissively. "I was using a common figure of speech. If I said 'let sleeping dogs lie' you wouldn't think I was calling your friend a dog, would you?"

"I'm not buying it," Walt said. "You know something, and I'm going to find out what it is."

"Don't waste any more of my time." Metwater left the room. Walt stared after him. The Prophet was going to be on guard now that he knew he was being watched, but that wouldn't keep Walt from finding out the truth.

When Walt emerged from the trailer, Hannah was waiting for him—along with Kiram. Walt ignored the bodyguard and addressed Hannah. "I thought you were with Phoenix." Before she could answer, Kiram stepped between them. "You aren't supposed to be together until the council meeting tonight," he said.

Walt studied the other man for a long moment. Kiram was clearly devoted to Metwater and his rules, but if the two of them hung around much longer he had no doubt one of them was going to lose his temper. "The Prophet has decided I'll be okay on my own." He nodded toward the door of the motor home. "If you don't believe me, go ask him."

Kiram looked from Walt to the motor home and back again. "You're trying to trick me."

"No trick," Walt said. "Go on and ask him. It's not as if you can't find me easily enough if it turns out I'm lying."

Kiram glared at Walt, then stormed up the steps and knocked. After a moment, he was admitted. Walt took Hannah's arm. "Let's get out of here," he said.

Hannah pulled him around behind the RV, out of sight of the rest of the camp. "When Phoenix went inside her trailer to get a diaper for Vicki, I walked away," she said. "I was getting worried about you. What did Metwater want?"

"He wanted to know what I told the police. And he wanted to know why we're here," he said. "He wasn't convinced we're true believers."

"What did you tell him?"

"The truth—or part of it. I told him we came here looking for Emily."

All the color left her cheeks and she released her hold on him. "What did he say?"

"He said she was here for a short time, but he didn't know what happened to her—or to her baby."

"Do you believe him?"

"Do you?"

"No." She glanced around, then pulled him farther into the woods, away from the campsite. "I think the people here are lying to us about a lot of things," she said. "And some of the things that might be the truth make me very uneasy. I think we should take the baby and get out of here as soon as possible."

She was still pale, and her hands shook as she smoothed back her hair. "What's got you so upset?" he asked.

"Phoenix told me Metwater has slept with most of the women here. She said she'd slept with him—that it was an honor. She said my turn would come—it doesn't matter that I'm married. Or, you know, that he thinks I'm married."

He smoothed his hand down her arm, trying to comfort her. "I'm not going to let him hurt you," he said.

"I won't be alone with him again," she said.

"Agreed. What else did Phoenix tell you? Did you learn anything more about Emily or Joy?"

She shook her head. "She only talked about the Prophet, and how he changed her life. And she said she had to give custody of Sophie to her parents for a while, but joining up with the Family made it possible for her to have Sophie with her again. But that didn't make a lot of sense to me. Would grandparents really turn over their granddaughter to live with a wandering bunch of modern-day hippies?"

"Maybe they would if they thought it was best for Sophie and for Phoenix."

"There's something else that's bothering me. Not anything Phoenix said, but something I saw."

"What is it?"

"You know how she always wears long sleeves?"

"I hadn't noticed."

"I had. All the other women wear tank tops or short sleeves—it can get pretty warm here during the day, especially in the kitchen. But Phoenix always stays covered up to her wrists. But this morning, when she reached for the baby, her sleeve pushed up and I saw that she has scars." She traced a line on the back of her arm, from elbow to wrist. "Thin lines. I wondered—could it be from drugs?"

"Maybe," Walt said. "Have you noticed any signs that she's using now?"

"No. I don't think she is. She says Daniel Metwater saved her life—do you think she means he helped her get off drugs?"

"I don't know."

She looked back toward the camp. "I don't like it here, and I can't shake the feeling there's a lot going on we don't know about. But maybe it's also possible that Metwater is doing some good, at least for some people."

"I guess no one is all good or all bad, but I still don't trust him."

"When can we leave and take Joy with us?"

"Soon," he said. "When the Rangers get here, I'm going to request a court order for us to take the baby into temporary custody, until a DNA test confirms her identity."

"Will they be able to get it?"

"I think so. In the meantime, I'd rather stay here to make sure they don't try to leave with her."

"I won't let them take her away," Hannah said. "When will you hear from the Rangers again?"

"They can't open up the grave until a forensic anthropologist can be on site. That might take a day or two. They'll want to see what's in there before they question anyone in the camp."

"In the meantime, we've got this council tonight," she said. "What do you think they'll do?"

"I think they'll make a lot of noise and try to scare us," he said. "Just remember they don't have any authority over us."

"That doesn't mean they won't try to hurt us—that they didn't hurt Emily, or Lucia."

"Serenity!" Phoenix raced up to them, her face flushed and out of breath. "There you are," she said, gasping. "I thought you had run away."

"I had to see Walt," Hannah said.

Phoenix glanced at him, then took both Hannah's hands in hers. "You shouldn't keep breaking the rules," the older woman said. "It will only go against you at council tonight."

Hannah pulled her hands free. "I won't blindly obey arbitrary rules that don't make sense," she said.

"Without rules, there's only chaos," Phoenix said.

"But rules have to have a larger purpose than merely controlling people," Walt said.

Phoenix shook her head and grabbed Hannah's hands again. "Please come back with me," she said. "Or I could get into trouble."

This time, Hannah didn't pull away. "All right," she said. "But Walt has to come with me."

"Where's Kiram?" Phoenix asked. She looked

around as if she expected the bearded young man to pop out from behind a tree.

"The Prophet and I talked and he agreed I didn't need a babysitter." Walt put his arm around Hannah again. "Hannah and I can stay with you this afternoon," he said. "And we'll try to keep out of trouble."

"Tell me another one," Phoenix said. "Men like you have trouble written all over them."

She turned and started walking away. Walt and Hannah followed. Hannah leaned in close. "She's right," she whispered. "You do look like a man who wouldn't shy away from trouble."

"Is that such a bad thing?" he asked.

"Oh, not at all." She squeezed his arm. "I'm beginning to think it's a very good thing."

THEY RETURNED TO Phoenix's trailer, where Sophie sat at the small table, surrounded by books, and Vicki played on a quilt on the floor. Hannah moved past Phoenix to scoop the baby up from the floor. "This is Vicki," she said, turning to Walt.

"Hey there, cutie." A huge grin split his face and before she could protest, he was lifting the baby from her arms and cradling her against him. Vicki stared up at him in wonder, then reached up one chubby hand to pat his cheek. "What do you think, little one?" he asked. "Do I look like trouble to you?"

Hannah's stomach quivered and her knees felt unsteady. The sight of this tough, rugged man being so tender with the baby stirred her emotions. Walt was trouble all right—a big disruption to the smooth path she had laid out for herself. She needed to focus on getting Joy safely home and building a stable life for the two of them. She didn't see how she could do that without Walt's help. But it had been so easy to move from wanting his help to wanting more.

"What are you studying?" Walt asked. Still cradling Vicki, he had moved over to the table and was looking down on the books scattered around Sophie.

"It's my homeschool correspondence course," she said. "It's supposed to be Introduction to Algebra, but I'm all confused."

"Maybe I can help." He leaned over her. "What are you having problems with?"

"You definitely need to have children soon." Phoenix moved to Hannah's side. "He's great with them."

"Yeah, he is." Judging from Sophie's smiles, his explanation of algebra was helping her, and Vicki seemed more than content to gaze up at him and gnaw on his thumb.

"Tell me about Vicki's mother," Hannah said, hoping she wasn't making a mistake asking the question.

Phoenix stiffened. "I'm Victory's mother."

Hannah squeezed the other woman's hand. "You've done a wonderful job of caring for her, but I heard her birth mother was a young woman who called herself Freedom."

"Who told you that?" Phoenix looked toward the table, where Walt now sat beside Sophie.

"In a camp this small, there are no secrets," Hannah said. "Someone told me that when we first came here. What can you tell me about Freedom?"

"She was a troubled young woman who was looking for peace," Phoenix said. "She hoped to find it here, but she had a hard time obeying the rules." She sighed. "She was a lot like you in that respect—always wanting reasons, not willing to simply be and accept."

"You really think she was like me?" Hannah had focused so long on the differences between her and her sister that she hadn't considered all the ways they might be alike.

"She wasn't as lucky as you in love." Phoenix's gaze shifted to Walt. "She said the man she had been engaged to marry was killed. She needed the love of a family to surround her and her baby, and she hoped to find that here."

"What about her own family?" Hannah's voice was strained from the tears she was fighting to hold back.

"She never talked about them. Sometimes it's easier to turn to strangers than to family—families know all your mistakes, and that can make them harder to put behind you."

And you know all your family's mistakes, which can be harder to forgive, Hannah thought. She recalled the last argument she had had with Emily, before her sister left to join Metwater's group.

She pushed the painful memory away. "What happened to Freedom?" she asked.

"She left us. It was for the best, since she wasn't happy here."

"But how could she leave her baby behind?" Hannah asked.

"I don't know," Phoenix said. "It struck me as out of character, but when people are desperately unhappy, they don't always act like themselves."

"Mind if I join you?" Walt returned to the living area.

"We were just talking about Freedom," Hannah said.

Phoenix frowned. "You told him?" she asked Hannah.

"He's my husband. Of course I told him." How easily the lie flowed off her lips. The longer she was with Walt, the easier it was to imagine him as her partner—which was crazy, considering how little time she had known him. Being thrown together like this, with the underlying current of danger, was obviously getting to her.

"What happened the day Freedom left?" Walt asked.

"She went with the Prophet to Denver," Phoenix said. "He was speaking there and he asked her to go along. He wanted to spend more time with her, to try to persuade her to stay with the Family."

"I thought he had told her she should leave," Hannah said. "That he was punishing her for wanting to run away."

Phoenix nibbled her thumbnail. "Well, yes, he had told her that, but he wanted to give her one more chance. He thought the trip to Denver, just the two of them, would help him persuade her to stay."

"She didn't take the baby with her?" Hannah asked.

"No. She left Victory with me." She took the child from Walt, who didn't protest. "I've taken care of her practically since she was born."

"Did the Prophet say what happened while they were in Denver?" Walt asked.

Phoenix smoothed the baby's curls. "He said Freedom decided to stay in the city and he came back without her."

"That didn't strike you as odd?" Walt asked. "That she didn't come back for her baby?"

"I thought she would, at first," Phoenix said. "But then..." She shrugged. "The Prophet said her mind was made up and he wasn't able to stop her from leaving. He doesn't keep people here against their will."

"So he would have been fine if she had taken Vicki with her when she left?" Hannah asked.

Phoenix stood. "I think the baby needs changing," she said, and disappeared into the back room before they could protest.

"Mom says the Prophet would have changed his mind about making Freedom leave her baby behind if she had come back for Victory." Sophie looked up from her books. "She refuses to believe he would ever do anything cruel."

"What do you think?" Walt turned to look at the girl.

She shrugged and doodled in the corner of her notebook. "I think people do cruel things all the time. Why should he be different?"

A knock on the door interrupted them. Hannah looked toward the back of the trailer, but Phoenix didn't emerge. The knocking persisted.

"I'll get it," Sophie said, but Walt got to the door before her.

He opened it and Agent Marco Cruz moved past him into the room. "I'm looking for a woman named Phoenix," he said. "We have questions for her related to the disappearance of Lucia Raton."

Chapter Twelve

Walt bit the inside of his cheek to keep from blurting out the questions Marco's announcement brought to mind. Of all the suspects Walt might have singled out as having something to do with Lucia's disappearance, Phoenix wouldn't have even made the list.

At Marco's words Phoenix emerged from the back bedroom, her face even paler than usual. She took one look at the officers, then thrust the baby into Hannah's arms and bolted for the door, but Michael Dance stepped in behind Marco and caught her. "Calm down, ma'am," he said, leading her back to the sofa. "We just need to ask you some questions."

"What is this about?" Sophie had moved from her place at the table and stood behind the two officers, eyes wide with fear.

"Hannah, maybe you should take Sophie and the baby and wait for Phoenix outside," Walt said.

"No." Hannah cradled the infant to her shoulder and beckoned Sophie to her side. "I won't leave Phoenix alone with three strange men." She glared at Walt, as if she blamed him for this turn of events. "Can't you see she's terrified?"

"Why don't we all sit down?" Marco moved farther into the room, while Michael stayed by the door. Phoenix wrapped her arms across her stomach, as if trying to make herself as small as possible. "Ma'am, do you want your friends to leave?" Marco asked.

Phoenix raised her head to look at Hannah. "I want Hannah to stay," she said.

"If Hannah stays, so do I." Walt crossed his arms over his chest.

"I'll take the baby," Sophie said. She reached for the infant and Hannah surrendered her. Then Sophie turned and fled from the trailer, shoving past Michael and slamming the door behind her.

Marco brought a chair from the table and set it in front of the sofa where Phoenix and Hannah now sat next to each other.

"What is this about?" Hannah asked. "Are you charging her with some crime?"

Walt frowned at her and shook his head. She needed to be quiet and let the Rangers do their job. But she looked away from him.

"Ma'am, before we start, I need to know your real name," Marco said.

"My name is Phoenix."

"That isn't the name you were born with," Marco said.

She glared at him. "Phoenix is my name."

Marco consulted his phone. "But weren't you born Anna Ingels?"

Hannah gasped. Walt recognized the name, too—Anna Ingels was the other witness on Emily Dietrich's will.

"Anna is dead," Phoenix said. "I left her behind when I came here."

Marco took something from his shirt pocket and handed it to her. "Isn't this your driver's license?" he asked. "The picture is yours and the name is Anna Ingels."

Walt leaned over to peer at the picture, which did indeed look like Phoenix. It was a Colorado license, showing an address in Denver, with an expiration date two years from now.

Phoenix clutched the license. "Where did you get this?" she asked.

"Our forensics team found it, along with some other items belonging to you, in a grave in the woods not far from here," Marco said.

Walt sent his fellow agent a sharp look. *What else did you find in that grave?* he wanted to ask, but knew he would have to wait for the answer.

Phoenix bowed her head. Hannah put her arm around the older woman and rubbed her shoulder.

"Why don't you tell us how your license ended up in that grave?" Marco said, his tone gentle.

"I buried the license, along with some clothes and books and other things," Phoenix said. "Anna's things. Part of my old life. I have a new life now. I'm a new person. I didn't need those reminders of what I used to be."

"What did you used to be?" Marco asked.

She raised her head to meet his gaze, her face a picture of misery. "I'm not that person anymore. The Prophet saved me. He changed me. I don't have to think about that life anymore," she said.

"We ran your license," Marco said. "You have a criminal record for possession of heroin and prostitution."

That explained the tracks on her arm, Walt thought. And maybe why she had lost custody of Sophie temporarily.

"That was Anna. It wasn't me. I'm not like that anymore."

"There's no crime in starting over," Hannah said. "And no crime in burying some old clothes and papers."

Marco ignored her and leaned toward Phoenix. "When did you bury those things?" he asked.

"A couple of weeks ago," she said. "The Prophet had a vision that we should divest ourselves of anything from the past that was holding us back. Some people burned items, or boxed them up and mailed them to their families. I held a funeral to say goodbye to my old self, and buried everything that belonged to Anna." She smiled and the light returned to her eyes.

"It was wonderful—like being reborn. I truly was a Phoenix, rising from the ashes of my former self."

"Tell us about Lucia Raton," Marco said. "When did she come to the camp?"

Phoenix sighed. "The Prophet said we shouldn't talk about Lucia. Especially not to the police."

"Lucia is missing," Marco said. "She could be dead. I need you to tell me about her. When was she in camp?"

The lines on Phoenix's forehead deepened. "I don't know. We don't keep track of time here." She looked around the trailer. "I don't even have a calendar."

"Guess. How long ago was she here?"

She considered the question a moment longer. The sound of someone laughing somewhere outside drifted through the open window, along with hammering—ordinary sounds of life in the camp in sharp contrast to the surreal atmosphere inside the trailer. "I buried Anna's things when the moon was full," she said. "Lucia was here a few days after that—maybe a week."

Marco typed the information into his phone. "How long was she here?" he asked.

"Only a day. Less than that, really. She didn't spend the night."

"You're sure about that?" Marco asked.

"I'm sure. The Prophet told her she had to leave because she was underage. She was only seventeen." Her expression grew troubled. "I hope she's okay. She seemed like a sweet girl—a little defiant and confused, but that's part of what being a teenager is about, isn't it?"

"Did you spend a lot of time with her while she was here?" Marco asked.

"No. She came around and introduced herself to me and some other women who were preparing dinner, but we didn't really talk."

Marco took something from his shirt pocket and held it out to her. It was a plastic evidence bag that contained a necklace—a locket on a blackened silver chain. "Do you recognize this?" he asked.

Phoenix shook her head. "It doesn't look familiar."

Marco pressed a catch on the side of the locket and it opened to reveal a photograph of a man and woman. "Who is that?" Phoenix asked.

"Read the inscription," Marco said.

She leaned closer and read. "'To Lucia. We love you. Mami and Papi.'"

"So the locket belongs to Lucia Raton?" Hannah asked.

"Her parents described it when they listed the things she was wearing the last time they saw her." Marco returned the evidence bag to his pocket. "Are you sure you don't remember it?"

Phoenix shook her head. "No. I only saw her for a few minutes."

"Was she with anyone else when she came here?" Michael Dance spoke for the first time from his position by the door. "Was there anyone she hung out with while she was here?"

"Not really." Walt sensed her hesitation; Marco must have, too.

"What is it?" Marco asked. "Was there someone she spent time with here?"

"Easy offered to give her a ride back into town," she said.

"Who is Easy?" Hannah asked before either of the officers could speak. "I haven't met anyone here by that name."

"He's not a member of the Family," Phoenix said. "He just visits sometimes. He delivers groceries or gives people rides if they need to go somewhere and don't have their own car. Sometimes he runs errands for the Prophet."

"What kind of errands?" Walt hadn't meant to speak, but he couldn't keep the question back.

Phoenix shrugged. "I don't know. He buys stuff he needs or takes him to the airport when he flies somewhere to give a talk."

"When was the last time you saw Easy?" Marco asked.

"A few days ago. I don't remember." She shifted. "What does any of this have to do with me? I'm sorry the girl is missing, but I can't help you."

She looked up as the door to the trailer opened. Michael whirled to face the newcomer, one hand on the duty weapon at his side. Daniel Metwater stepped into the trailer. His hair was wet and he smelled of soap. He wore the same loose linen trousers he usually favored, and a flowing tunic of the same white linen. Walt thought of it as his official Prophet uniform. "What is going on here?" Metwater demanded, taking in the scene.

Marco stood and faced the newcomer. The door was still open and Sophie, carrying the baby, slipped past the officers and joined her mother on the sofa. The girl must have summoned the Prophet to help her mother. Kiram followed her, taking his place behind Metwater, his expression sullen, as usual. The small trailer was too crowded, and the air fairly crackled with tension. Walt thought of the gun in his ankle holster and hoped he wouldn't have to use it. He took a step closer to Hannah, prepared to shove her to the floor if bullets started flying.

"We're investigating the disappearance of a young woman who visited your camp shortly before she disappeared," Marco said.

"We had nothing to do with that," Metwater said.

"Why did you lie to us about having seen Lucia Raton?" Michael asked. "What are you trying to hide?"

"She was here for only a few hours," Metwater said. "And she was fine when she left here."

"Then why lie?" Marco asked.

"I'm entitled to my privacy. And you're trespassing in my home. You need to leave."

"This is public land," Marco said. "You are camping here because you have a permit, but that doesn't give you the right to exclude anyone—especially not officers of the law who are conducting an investigation."

"Why didn't you want us to know about the grave in that clearing?" Michael asked.

"I don't have to answer your questions." Metwater looked sullen, and less handsome and in-control than usual. "You need to leave."

Marco ignored the order, deliberately turning his back to Metwater to face Phoenix once more. "We found Lucia's locket in the grave with your belongings," he told her. "Can you explain how it got there?"

IF SHE WAS feigning shock, she was doing an amazing job, Hannah thought as Phoenix stared up at Marco. "That's impossible," she said. "I buried those things before Lucia ever visited the camp."

"Is there anyone who can confirm that?" Marco asked. "Anyone who helped you with the burial?"

She shook her head. "No. I did it alone. It was important that I do it alone."

"Did you tell anyone what you planned to do?" Marco asked. "Could someone have followed and seen you?"

"I only told the Prophet," Phoenix answered. "And why would someone have followed me?"

Hannah hated seeing the other woman so distressed. "Did you find anything else in the grave that belonged to Lucia?" she asked.

"The forensics team is still sorting through their findings," Marco said.

"You're wasting your time here," Metwater said. "You need to leave."

"We'll go, after we've questioned Mr. and Mrs. Morgan." He motioned to Walt and Hannah. "If you two will come with me, please."

Kiram moved to block the door. "Why do you want to talk to them?" he asked.

"We think it's a little suspicious that they showed up here about the time Lucia disappeared," Marco said.

Even though she knew the words were a lie, Hannah felt a tremor of fear. How much worse must Phoenix feel, being accused by these men who had so much power to destroy her life? She squeezed the older woman's hand, then stood and prepared to follow Walt and the others out of the trailer.

A hand on her shoulder stopped her. Metwater moved close to her—too close. His gaze locked to hers and he smoothed his hand down her arm in a possessive way that sent a shiver up her spine. "Don't be too long," he said. "You have to prepare for tonight's council."

Walt took her hand and tugged her toward the door. They followed Marco and Michael a short distance away, down a path that led into the woods along the creek. The noise of the water rushing over the rocks was a soothing contrast to the tension knotting tighter inside her with each passing minute.

"You're on the wrong track here," she said when the two lawmen stopped and faced her and Walt. "Phoenix couldn't have had anything to do with Lucia's disappearance. She's not the type to harm someone else."

"I got the impression she would do just about anything for Metwater," Marco said. "You heard her—he saved her life."

She looked at the ground, unable to think of a response. Phoenix did have a blind spot when it came to the Prophet.

"How did that locket get in the grave if she didn't put it there?" Walt asked.

"Don't know." Michael leaned against a tree, his posture relaxed. "What do you make of her story about burying her past?"

"I believe it," Walt said. "It's the kind of thing Metwater would preach. They're very big into rituals and ceremonies around here."

"What is this council he mentioned?" Marco asked.

"Some kind of meeting to decide on the appropriate punishment for me disobeying Metwater's orders and going to you guys to report the grave," Walt said.

"Punishment?" Michael asked. "What kind of punishment?"

"I don't know." Walt turned to Hannah. "Have you heard anything?"

"Phoenix said it will probably be extra work or something like that—something to impress upon us the importance of putting the Family ahead of ourselves. We have to prove we're serious about our intentions to become one of them."

"How serious are you?" Marco asked. "Why not just leave now? You've probably learned all you're going to learn at this point."

"We know Phoenix's baby is really my niece," Hannah said. "She told us this afternoon—right before you arrived—that the baby belonged to a woman who called herself Freedom. And Phoenix's real name on my sister's will proves she was at the hospital when the baby was born."

"There's still the problem of Metwater's name as the father on the birth certificate," Walt said. "He can fight any attempt to gain custody."

"Not if we have a DNA test proving paternity," Hannah said. "And not if we prove he was involved in Emily's death." She turned to Marco. "Phoenix said Metwater took Emily to Denver with him and came back without her. He told everyone here that she had left—she had abandoned her baby. Why would he lie about her having died in the hospital, unless he had something to do with her death?"

"He lies about a lot of things," Michael said. "But in most cases, lying itself isn't a crime."

"Why didn't you ask Phoenix about the will?" Hannah asked.

The two officers looked at each other. "We were so focused on the search for Lucia we weren't thinking about your sister's will," Marco said.

"Were you able to get the warrant for the DNA test on the baby?" she asked.

Another look passed between them. "Not yet," Marco admitted.

"I can't leave camp without the baby," she said.

"Taking her without the court order could backfire if Metwater decides to press charges," Walt said. "Child Welfare and Protection has already indicated they're on his side. They could ask the court to award temporary custody to Metwater, pending the outcome of the DNA test, and while we're waiting on results, he could leave the area with the baby."

"I won't risk it," Hannah said. "I have to stay here until I can legally take her away."

Michael straightened. "We'll push harder for the court order. In the meantime, see if you can find out anything that would link Metwater to Lucia's disappearance."

"We also need to find this Easy fellow and interview him," Marco said. He clapped a hand on Walt's shoulder. "Let us know if you discover anything useful. And try to stay out of trouble."

"Right," Walt said. He took Hannah's arm and they walked silently back to camp. She fought the urge to lean into him, to let his presence shield her from the anxiety coiling inside her. Maybe it was seeing

Phoenix so frightened, or maybe this was simply the emotional side effect of digging so deeply into Emily's last days, but she felt overwhelmed and a little out of control. As if sensing her struggle, Walt put his arm around her. "It's going to be all right," he said. "It will all be over soon."

Chapter Thirteen

"Phoenix is waiting for you," Kiram told Hannah as she and Walt approached Phoenix's trailer. "She will help you prepare for tonight." He motioned to Walt. "You come with me."

Walt started to protest, but Hannah interrupted. "It will be all right," she said, repeating the words of comfort he had given her. She kissed his cheek. "I'll see you soon."

Much as she would have liked to stay with Walt, she would learn more from Phoenix without him there. She made her way back to Phoenix's trailer and found her laying an assortment of supplies on the table—soap, paints, hair ribbons and a simple white garment Hannah suspected was sewn from a bedsheet. "What is all this?" she asked, surveying the array.

"This is for tonight." Phoenix smiled at her. "You want to look your best for the council." She picked up the soap. "First, bathe with this. Then we'll do your hair and makeup."

The soap was obviously homemade and smelled astringent—not the moisturizing bar Hannah preferred. But she didn't argue, and walked with Phoenix to the outdoor shower someone had built, utilizing a plastic drum to store water that was heated by the sun. After a quick soap and rinse, they walked back to the trailer, where Phoenix seated Hannah at the table and began combing out her hair, humming to herself.

"I told the officers I thought you were innocent," Hannah said after a moment. "I'm sure you didn't have anything to do with that girl's disappearance."

"I have faith they'll learn that soon enough." She picked up a ribbon and began braiding it into a section of Hannah's hair.

"When I heard your real name—your old name—I realized it was familiar to me," she said.

Phoenix's fingers stopped moving. "Did we know each other before?" she asked, her tone puzzled.

"You were one of the witnesses on Emily—Freedom's—will." She waited for Phoenix to ask how she knew about the will, but the other woman merely went back to braiding Hannah's hair.

"She asked me to sign some papers for her, so I did," Phoenix said. "A nurse from the hospital was there and she signed, too."

"Why did she decide to write a will?" Hannah asked. "What was she afraid of?"

"Oh, she wasn't afraid. Not exactly."

"But she was upset about something?" Hannah

prodded. "Why else would she be so anxious to have a will that she wrote it right there in the hospital?"

"She had had a fight with the Prophet. That upset her."

Hannah turned to look at her. "A fight? What about? Did he threaten her?"

"The Prophet doesn't threaten—he disciplines. And only because we need it. Just as a loving father disciplines his children."

Hannah could guess where those words had come from. "How did he discipline Emily?" she asked, stomach cramping in anticipation of the answer.

"I don't know. And I don't know what they argued about, either. That was between Freedom and the Prophet."

"I don't think an adult has the right to 'discipline' another adult," Hannah said.

"You just don't understand because you haven't experienced it." She picked up another ribbon and began braiding another section of Hannah's hair. "For instance, when I first came here, I was still trying to get off heroin. The Prophet locked me up in his motor home and looked after me while I went through withdrawal. He wouldn't let me leave, even though I tried to run away. Some people might have seen it as cruel that he kept me prisoner that way, but he saved my life."

"Emily wasn't a drug addict," Hannah said. She took a deep breath, reining in her anger. "She was a grieving young woman with a new baby. She didn't need to be punished for anything."

"I'm sure the Prophet had his reasons," Phoenix said. "I've never known him to be wrong."

Hannah turned to face her once more. "Do you think he's going to punish me for Walt going to the police?" she asked.

Phoenix brushed a lock of hair from Hannah's forehead. "He likes you. I can tell by the way he looks at you. You're going to be one of his favorites. Whatever he does, it will only be because he cares for you."

Hannah felt sick to her stomach at the words. She didn't want Daniel Metwater's brand of caring. She had to find a way to safely leave here, and to take Joy with her. *What about Walt?* a voice in the back of her mind whispered. *Will you take him with you, too—or leave him behind?*

"I'M NOT GOING to walk out there in front of a whole camp full of people naked." Walt folded his arms and glared at the scrap of cloth Kiram was holding out for him to put on.

"Everyone else will be dressed this way," Kiram said. "It's to show we have nothing to hide from each other."

Walt took the loincloth. He definitely wouldn't be able to hide a weapon in this getup. He would bet Kiram and Metwater's other "bodyguards" would be wearing their knives along with this primitive excuse for a Speedo. But he didn't see any way to get out of wearing the thing if he wanted to avoid raising further suspicion. "I'll wear it," he said. "But I'm putting my regular clothes back on as soon as this is over."

Kiram shrugged. "What did those cops want with you and your wife?" he asked.

Walt had been waiting for this to come up. "They asked if we knew the missing girl—if we had ever met her or seen her or knew anything about her."

"What did you tell them?"

He pretended to examine the loincloth. "We told them the truth—we didn't know anything."

"Seems like they could have asked you all that when you told them about the grave site."

"Yeah, well, they didn't." He stuffed the loincloth into his pocket. "I guess I'll go back to my tent and change."

"You can change at my place." He pointed to the shack behind them.

"What do I do with my clothes?"

"Leave them here. They'll be fine with me."

And Kiram would be going through his things as soon as Walt was out of sight. "Okay." He headed for the shack. He'd have to find a hiding place for his gun while he was at the council—someplace Kiram wasn't likely to look.

He stripped off quickly, folded his clothes and left them on the end of Kiram's cot. He thought about hiding the weapon under the bed, but ended up stashing it behind a rafter overhead. In the dim light, it would be almost impossible to see. Then he took a few minutes to poke around in the room. Kiram had a small collection of manga novels and another of porn magazines, stashed in a wooden crate that served as his bedside table. He had a wardrobe of mostly shorts and cargo pants and T-shirts; a toolbox with an assortment of screwdrivers, wrenches and a hammer; and a dartboard with only three darts. A sagging, faded sofa sat against one wall.

Walt eyed the footlocker that sat at the end of the cot. He wished he had the time to check the contents of it, but he didn't dare risk it right now.

The door opened and Kiram stepped in. "What's taking so long?" he asked. "You'd better not be messing with my stuff."

"It took me a while to figure out how to get this thing on." Walt snapped the waistband of the loincloth, which was a little too breezy for comfort.

"Come on, let's go." He stepped aside and motioned for Walt to move ahead of him.

A soft drizzle had begun to fall—enough moisture to make everything damp and uncomfortable, but not enough to get them really wet. The murmur of voices drifted through the trees, swelling as they neared the center of the camp. A bonfire blazed, flames bright against the surrounding blackness, popping wood sending out showers of sparks like fireflies. It looked to Walt as if everyone in camp had gathered, most dressed in the same kind of faux-native garb he and Kiram wore. The crowd parted as he followed Kiram to a spot by the fire, and he looked across the circle and saw Hannah with Phoenix and Sophie.

For the briefest moment, he couldn't breathe, as if he had forgotten how. Her hair was down, spilling around her shoulders in a mass of tiny braids threaded with purple and pink and blue ribbons. She wore a simple sheath which, though it covered her from her collarbone to just above the knees, did nothing to hide her feminine curves. If anything, it made him more aware than ever of his attraction to her. He wanted her, yes, but he also wanted to protect her and champion her and work alongside her.

Kiram prodded him in the side. "Close your mouth and stop gaping," he said. "You'd think you'd never seen your wife before."

A clap of thunder shook the air and a murmur swept through the crowd like a wave, and the mass of people parted to reveal Daniel Metwater striding toward the fire. Walt wondered how long he had waited in the background for that thunderclap to announce his entrance—he doubted it was merely coincidence. Like most of the other men he, too, wore a loincloth, revealing muscular legs and the body of someone who spent a lot of time working out. His chest and face were painted in primitive symbols rendered in red, white and black—his eyes circled in white, a black streak down his nose, and more lines on his cheek and chin. It reminded Walt of a poor copy of an African tribal mask he had once seen in a museum. The effect was eerie, firelight flickering on his familiar, yet not familiar visage.

Metwater raised both hands over his head and the crowd quieted. "Thank you all for gathering with me tonight," he said, his voice booming in the sudden silence. "Thank you for recognizing the importance of coming together as a family, and of working as one to build something beautiful—something the outside world doesn't understand."

Walt recognized the technique—build cohesiveness in a group by pitting the members against an outside enemy—a mysterious "them."

"We are here tonight to consider the fate of two who have petitioned to join us," Metwater continued. "Serenity—" He gestured to Hannah. "And Walter."

Walt was sure the use of names neither he nor Hannah preferred was deliberate, another way of saying *I'm the one in charge here.* "They have expressed a desire to become part of our family, but their actions show they yet lack the discipline and commitment required to build a strong unit," Metwater said.

Walt caught Hannah's eye across the circle. She gave him a half smile, then made a face at Metwater. *Attagirl.*

"I have spent much time in meditation on their fate, and I have received a vision."

Walt watched the faces of those around him as

they listened to Metwater. They stared fixedly at him, some almost trancelike as his words rose and fell, his voice having the rhythm and cadence of a hypnotist. He was good, Walt had to admit. But if you had to trick people into listening to you, how good of a leader could you really be?

Metwater spent some time describing his vision—something to do with a figure all in white—an angel—coming to him with a tablet, on which was written the solution to their problem. Were people really buying this? Apparently so, as they began to murmur and nod their heads in agreement.

Suddenly, Metwater reached out and grabbed Hannah's hand and yanked her to his side. Walt hadn't even realized he had lunged forward until Kiram pulled him back. The blade of Kiram's knife pressed to his throat. "I wouldn't make another move if I were you," the bearded man said.

Walt probably could have fought off the other man. He'd been trained in self-defense and was confident of his abilities. But he couldn't fight off a whole camp full of men, and the way this bunch was hanging on Metwater's every word, if the Prophet had commanded them to kill Walt, they wouldn't have hesitated to fall on him like a pack of rabid dogs.

Hannah tried to pull away from Metwater, but he held her fast. She settled for glaring at him. Clearly, she hadn't fallen under his spell like so many others. "My vision told me to welcome Serenity to our fold with open arms," Metwater said. "She has a true gentle spirit and will be an asset to us. With proper guidance, I believe she will come to be a revered and respected member of the group."

Hannah's expression didn't soften. Walt imagined she was grinding her teeth to keep from reminding Metwater that her name wasn't Serenity and she wasn't interested in his guidance.

"As of tonight, Serenity will live with me and I will take personal responsibility for her education and training."

A murmur rose from the crowd. Phoenix clapped her hands together, apparently thrilled. Hannah paled and tried, in vain, to pull away from Metwater. *That does it*, Walt thought. They were leaving tonight. He wasn't going to give Metwater a chance to "educate" Hannah, whatever form that might take.

At last Metwater handed Hannah off to Phoenix again. "Now to the question of Walter," he said. The crowd shifted to stare at Walt, who glared back.

"I fear, and my vision confirmed, that he does not have the proper spirit of cooperation that would allow him to be a valued member of our group," Metwater said. "He has shown a blatant disregard for our rules and an unhealthy defiance."

Or maybe just a healthy skepticism that you would have anyone's benefit but your own in mind, Walt thought.

"For the good of the Family, Walter must be banished," Metwater declared.

"No!" The cry came from Hannah, who was being held back by Phoenix and another woman.

"Fine by me," Walt said. "I'll leave tonight." And he would be back before morning with a team of Rangers to free Hannah and arrest Metwater for kidnapping.

Metwater ignored him. "In order that he may learn a valuable lesson, and have time to reconsider his rebellious attitude, he will undergo a trial."

"I've had enough of this nonsense," Walt muttered.

Kiram took a firmer hold on him. "Don't try anything," the bearded man whispered.

Metwater turned and strode toward him. There was nothing natural in his movements—he was a performer on stage, playing to his audience. He stopped in front of Walt. "You will be taken out into the wilderness. From there, you can make your own way back to the world. You are never to come here again."

"I have my bike," Walt said.

"No. I have your bike." Metwater smiled. "Or rather, you are leaving it behind for your lovely wife."

"You can't do this," Walt said.

"If you could speak with others who have tried to defy me, you would learn that I can." He turned his back on Walt and crossed the circle to Hannah.

"I won't stay with you," she said. "I'm leaving with my husband."

"I am your husband now," Metwater said. "And your father and your brother and all you need." The words were beyond cheesy, but the frightening thing was, Metwater had managed to brainwash these people into believing them. He took Hannah's hand and held fast when she tried to turn away.

Walt shoved aside Kiram's hand, not caring that the knife grazed his arm, drawing blood. "Let her go!" he shouted.

His eyes met Hannah's, and behind her panic he saw strength, and then alarm. "Walt, look out!" she cried, and then he felt a sharp pain at the back of his head, and everything went black.

Chapter Fourteen

Hannah couldn't believe this was happening. Up until now everything about the evening—from the ridiculous dress-up clothes to Metwater's bombastic speech—had seemed like a silly game. It hardly seemed credible that anyone could get away with things like kidnapping and banishment in front of a crowd of people in this day and age.

But they were in an almost roadless wilderness area, far from other people and laws and even cell phones. That isolation—and his followers' willingness to be hypnotized by his words—gave Metwater more power than he might otherwise have had.

But she wasn't going to allow him to have power over her. "Stop!" she shouted, as two men carried Walt's inert body away from the fire, into the darkness. She kicked and clawed at the men who had moved in to help the women contain her, but they only tightened their hold.

"Serenity! Hannah! You need to calm down."

Phoenix grasped her hand and patted it, her face twisted in concern. "You don't need to get so upset."

"They hurt Walt," she said, fighting a mixture of rage and dismay.

"I'm sure they didn't." Phoenix squeezed her hand. "He'll be fine. Meanwhile, you've been given a great honor."

Hannah stared at her friend, confused.

"You're going to live with the Prophet." Phoenix stroked her hair. "He rarely takes such an interest in anyone. It's really a privilege."

Hannah winced. "He can take his privilege and stick it where the sun doesn't shine!"

"Freedom was the same way when he chose her," Phoenix said. "Don't make the same mistake she did and fight with him. In the end it will only do you more harm than good."

"He did this to my sister?" Hannah stared at her. "He forced himself on her?"

Phoenix looked flustered. "I don't know about your sister. I was talking about Freedom."

"Freedom was my sister," Hannah said. "Her name was Emily Dietrich, and her daughter's name is Joy. I have Joy's birth certificate, and the will you witnessed. I know."

Phoenix shook her head, as if trying to clear it. "Have you seen her? Spoken to her? Did you ask her why she left her baby?"

"She didn't leave her." Hannah was crying now,

tears streaming down her face, even as the two men who held her dragged her toward Metwater's RV. "Emily couldn't come back to her baby because she's dead," she said.

"I don't understand," Phoenix said.

"My sister—Emily—Freedom—is dead," Hannah said. "She died in Denver, when she went there with the Prophet. I believe he killed her."

Phoenix stopped at the bottom of the steps leading to the motor home's door. "That isn't possible," she said. "He told us she had left."

"She would never have left her baby," Hannah said. "You know that."

"I don't—" Phoenix began.

"Come on." One of the women had opened the door to Metwater's RV and held it while the men dragged Hannah backward up the steps. They must have heard what she told Phoenix, but they showed no reaction. "You don't want to keep the Prophet waiting," the woman said.

They dragged Hannah into the RV, which appeared to be empty. If Daniel Metwater was there, he wasn't showing his face. They shoved her into a room and the lock clicked behind her. She stood for a moment, catching her breath and taking stock of her surroundings. The room contained a futon and a single chair. One window. She dragged the chair over to the window, climbed up on it and tried to force up the sash. It wouldn't budge.

"You won't get out that way."

Metwater stood in the doorway. He had removed the paint and the loincloth, and changed back into his loose linen trousers. "The window is nailed shut from the outside," he said. "And there's mesh over the pane so you can't break the glass." He moved closer to her and held out his hand. "Come down from there and let's talk."

He led her to the futon and pushed her down, then sat beside her. "You're even prettier than your sister," he said.

"What did you do to Emily?" she asked.

"I tried to help her, but she wouldn't accept my help." His smile sent a cold shiver through her stomach.

"She didn't need your help," she said.

"You say that because you want to believe that you were all she needed. But if that had been true, she wouldn't have left you and come to us."

His words were like a knife to her heart. No matter how long she lived, she would never stop believing she had somehow failed her sister. "What did you do to her?" she asked. "Why did she die?"

"An unfortunate accident," he said. He reached for her and she pulled away.

"I want to know what happened in Denver," she said. "Why did my sister die alone?"

He sat back, his expression hard. "I took her to the hospital. There was nothing else I could do for her."

She shivered, struck by his coldness. "You could have stayed with her. She was probably terrified."

He said nothing.

"Why did you lie and tell everyone she had run away?" she asked.

"There was no sense upsetting the rest of the Family. I don't believe in dwelling on negatives. What's important is the future." He reached for her again, but she pushed him away.

He scowled. "You're upset," he said. "But I can be patient—for a while." He stood. "We'll talk again in the morning."

"What did you do with Walt?"

"I didn't do anything," he said.

"That's how you operate, isn't it?" Anger made her bold. "You have other people do your dirty work for you."

"Go to sleep," he said. "We'll talk in the morning."

He shut off the light and closed the door. Her instinct was to run after him, to pound on the door and shout for him to let her out. But no one would pay any attention to her, least of all Metwater. She sank onto the futon and glared at the shut window. She had to figure out a way to get out of here. She had to find Walt, and together they had to get Joy and take her to safety.

She thought of Emily, trapped in this same room, missing her baby and desperate to escape. She hadn't been lucky enough to get away. Maybe she hadn't been strong enough. But Hannah would be strong enough for both of them. She would take care of her sister's child. Failure wasn't an option.

WALT CAME TO lying flat on his back in the darkness. He was wet and cold, and something hard was digging into his spine. Groaning, he shoved himself into a sitting position and wiped dripping water out of his eyes. It was raining—a steady drizzle that ran in rivulets across the rocky ground around him. He could make out little in the darkness, except that he was somewhere away from camp, presumably in the wilderness.

He was still wearing the stupid loincloth and was barefoot. He wouldn't get far in this country full of rocks and thorns in such a state of undress. Of course, before very long he'd probably die of hypothermia, what with the rain soaking him and nighttime temperatures in the fifties. Or he'd starve or die of thirst, since the rainwater would dry up in a matter of hours once the sun rose. Metwater was counting on that. It was a good way to kill someone without actually having to pull the trigger. If the body was found later, Metwater could always claim Walt had wandered into the wilderness on his own.

But he didn't have to get far—he only had to get back to camp. He wasn't going to die out here. He would rescue Hannah, recover his clothes and his bike, and head back to Ranger headquarters. Then Metwater would discover how hard paybacks could be.

He struggled to his feet, swaying a little, dizzy from the pounding in his head. He ran his fingers over the knot at the back of his skull, his hair sticky from what he imagined was drying blood. He took a few steps, wincing as rocks dug into his feet. He stumbled over something—a log or a boulder—and fell, hitting the ground hard and cursing loudly. The only answer was the steadily falling rain.

This wasn't going to work. It was too dark to see where he was going. He'd have to wait until it was light. Then he could take his bearings and determine the most likely route back to the camp. Otherwise, he might break his leg or stumble over a cliff. He wouldn't be any help to Hannah, lying at the bottom of a ravine.

Moving carefully, hands outstretched like a blind man, feet shuffling along, he made his way to a tree and huddled at the base of the trunk. Knees drawn up and arms wrapped around his legs, he tried to warm himself. Distraction—that was what he needed. He just had to stick it out here a few more hours. He started by thinking of all the ways he would make Metwater and Kiram pay for their treatment of him and Hannah. He had compiled a long list of possible charges against them, from kidnapping and assault to fraud and violating the county burn bans.

The idea was satisfying, but it couldn't keep his

thoughts from straying to his chief worry—not fear for his own life or concern that he might not find the camp again, but worry for Hannah. He felt physically ill, knowing she might be in danger and he was out here, powerless.

She's tough, he reminded himself. *She isn't afraid to stand up to Metwater. She's smart, too.* She was the most amazing woman he knew, and out here in the darkness, with nothing between him and his feelings, he realized he had fallen in love with her. It wasn't something he had intended to happen, but there it was. He'd lost his heart to a woman who lived in another state, who was focused on making a new life with her orphaned niece and who clearly had no room in her life for an ordinary cop.

HANNAH MOVED THE chair from the window and wedged it under the bedroom doorknob. She'd have to remove it eventually, but at least Metwater wouldn't be able to come into the room while she slept.

If sleep were even possible. She lay down on the futon, her mind racing with thoughts of her sister, of Joy, of Metwater—and of Walt.

Where was he right now? Had Kiram taken him out into the desert and killed him? Or left him to die? Her throat constricted and she swallowed tears. How had the lawman come to mean so much to her in such a short time? He wasn't like any of the other men she had known—he didn't try to change her or expect anything of her or judge her choices. He didn't need her for anything, yet when she was with him she felt stronger and smarter and more confident. Time spent with him seemed better than time spent alone—and that had never been the case with anyone else.

Her breath caught, and she sat up in bed. Was she falling in love with Walt? Was that even possible when she had known him such a short time? She didn't want a man in her life—didn't need one. She had work and Joy and so much going on. How could that leave any room for a relationship?

She tossed and turned until the window changed from a square of black to a square of silvery gray. She returned to the window and stood on tiptoe to see out. No one moved out there at this hour. Not that she would expect to see anyone at any time of day, really. The back of the RV looked out onto a choked mass of trees and underbrush that bordered the creek.

She shoved at the window sash again, and scowled at the wire mesh that covered the glass. If only she was strong enough to throw up the sash despite the nails. Would it help if she had listened to her friends and taken up weight training?

A scraping noise outside the RV made her freeze. Heart racing, she rose on tiptoe again and took a look outside. A scream stuck in her throat as a figure loomed up on the other side of the window. She jumped back, then sagged with relief when she recognized Phoenix. The other woman held up a hammer, then used it to pry the nails from the sill. Moments later, the sill shot up and Phoenix leaned her head in.

"I couldn't sleep," she said. "I've been thinking about what you said—about your sister. Do you think the Prophet really killed her?"

Hannah wanted to suggest Phoenix help her get out of the RV without Metwater knowing, and then they could have this discussion, but she couldn't be sure whose side the other woman was on. She was such an ardent fan of the Prophet that the odds seemed about even that she would alert him of any attempt Hannah made to escape. Better to try to win her over to Hannah's point of view. She moved closer to the window and kept her voice low. "I don't know. She died in the hospital emergency room, of an asthma attack."

Phoenix looked thoughtful. "I remember she had an inhaler she used. She said she was going to get her prescription filled while she and the Prophet were in Denver."

"Maybe he didn't let her fill it."

"Why wouldn't he? I mean, it wasn't as if she used it very much at all."

"No, but stress can make asthma worse. If she and the Prophet were fighting, she would be stressed."

Phoenix frowned. "But that doesn't mean he killed her."

"No. But he left her at the hospital alone." Hannah struggled to hold back her anger. "And he lied to you and everyone else here about what happened to her."

"That's what troubles me most," Phoenix said. "Why would he do that?"

"I don't know. Help me down, will you?"

"I'm not sure I should help you leave."

"I don't want to be here. The Prophet is holding me against my will. Do you think that's right?"

Phoenix hesitated so long, Hannah began to despair. Maybe she should rush the window and try to move past the other woman. "He's not going to like you leaving," Phoenix said. "He'll probably send Kiram and others after you. They might even try to hurt you."

"I know. They might already have hurt Walt. But I have to risk it. I can't stay here."

"All right, I'll help you," Phoenix said. "But wait just a minute. I'll be right back—I promise."

Before Hannah could protest, Phoenix shut the window and climbed down the ladder. By the time Hannah had the window open again, Phoenix had laid the ladder on the ground and left. Hannah moaned softly. The sun was already higher in the sky. She had no idea if Metwater was an early riser, but what if he was and decided to pay her a visit?

THE RAIN SLACKED off and Walt fell into a doze. When he woke again, stiff and cold, the sky was pale with the first hint of dawn. Standing, he pushed out of the underbrush and studied his surroundings. Nothing about this area looked familiar. Maybe if he had been on the job longer he would be more familiar with the wilderness backcountry, but his work thus far had kept him mostly in the national park and along roads. Before him spread a landscape of brown dirt, red and gray rock, and clumps of gnarled trees and sagebrush.

He tried to retrace his steps from the night before, and found the place where Kiram had left him, drag marks in the mud clearly showing where the bearded man had dumped him. Following the drag marks, he came to the impression of tires, showing where Kiram had parked his vehicle. The treads led away from the parking spot in a clear path across the prairie.

Heart pounding, Walt moved faster, trotting now, ignoring the pain in his feet as he followed the faint impressions in the mud. With a little luck, he'd be able to follow these tracks all the way back to the road, and from there to the camp.

An hour later, just as the first hints of pale blue were showing in the sky, Walt crept into the woods on the outskirts of camp. Moving stealthily, seeking cover behind trees and the random piles of junk that had accumulated among the trailers, tents and shacks, he peered out at the center gathering area. No one was moving about yet. A tendril of smoke rose from the remains of last night's bonfire, and the air smelled of wet ashes and earth.

Satisfied that no one was about, he made his way to his tent and quickly dressed. His only shoes were in Kiram's shack, along with his gun. Not wanting to be unarmed, he crept to the camp kitchen and found a knife. Suddenly ravenous, he ate some bread and cheese he found, then stuffed his pockets with several energy bars. Then he headed for Metwater's RV.

Barging into the motor home would be a bad idea. Reports he had read at Ranger headquarters indicated Metwater owned at least one firearm, and Walt couldn't be sure the Prophet was in the RV alone.

Alone except for Hannah. Walt needed to find out where she was, then make a plan for freeing her. He crept around the motor home, listening for any sign of movement inside. Most of the windows were too high up for him to see into, and he couldn't tell much about the layout of the vehicle. He thought the bedroom or bedrooms were to the left of the door, but he couldn't be sure.

He stood at the back of the RV, considering his next move, when a voice from behind him made him freeze. "Walt! You're not supposed to be here."

Slowly, he turned and stared at Phoenix. She stood at the far end of the RV, paler than ever in the early-morning light. And was that a bow and arrow she had trained on him?

HANNAH LEANED HER head against the windowsill and listened for any signs of movement in the other parts of the RV. If she heard anyone coming, she would jump out the window. Maybe she'd get lucky and wouldn't break any bones.

She wasn't sure how many minutes had passed when she heard voices outside. She looked toward the end of the RV where they seemed to be coming from and gasped as she recognized Walt and Phoenix. He was standing with his hands over his head, and Phoenix was pointing something at him. Hannah craned her neck for a closer look and gasped. Was that a bow and arrow?

THE BOW AND arrow Phoenix held looked crude, but effective. Walt had no doubt the arrow could do serious damage, especially at such close range. "I'm here to help Hannah," he said.

"Phoenix, what are you doing?"

Walt didn't dare turn around, but he recognized Hannah's voice behind him. Phoenix shifted her gaze to over his shoulder. "He's not supposed to be here," she said.

"No, I'm supposed to be dead," Walt said. "Kiram took me out into the desert and left me to die of exposure or thirst or whatever it took."

"How did you get back?" Phoenix asked.

"He was too stupid to realize his truck would leave tracks in the fresh mud. As soon as it was light enough, I followed his trail back to camp."

"Could we discuss this later?" Hannah asked.

Phoenix lowered the bow, and together she and Walt hurried to the window where Hannah waited. He spotted the ladder and propped it against the RV, then together he and Phoenix helped Hannah climb out.

She wrapped her arms around his neck. "I was so worried about you," she said.

He held her close, unable to let go. "Are you okay?" he asked, studying her face.

She nodded. "I am. Especially now." She turned to Phoenix. "What are you doing with that bow and arrow?"

"Some guys made them a while back to hunt rabbits. They didn't have any luck but since you said you were leaving camp, I thought you might want one. You know, for self-defense."

"Is that why you left—to get something to help me protect myself?"

Bright color flooded Phoenix's normally pale cheeks. "I wedged the front door of the motor home shut. If the Prophet saw you escaping, I wanted to slow down his pursuit."

Hannah moved from Walt's arms into Phoenix's. "Thank you," she said, and kissed the older woman's cheek.

"We need to leave before everyone wakes up," Walt reminded her.

"First we have to get Joy—Vicki." She squeezed Phoenix's arm. "She has to go with us."

"No!"

Walt flinched at Phoenix's loud cry, and looked around to see if anyone had heard.

"Yes," Hannah said. "Emily—Freedom—wanted me to have the baby. She said so in her will."

"If the Prophet finds out I gave her to you, he'll punish me." Phoenix looked on the verge of tears.

"Then tell him I stole her."

Phoenix shook her head, tears streaming down her face. Walt clenched his jaw, hating how helpless he felt. He wanted to tell Hannah to leave the baby—that they would come back for her later. But he might as well have told her to leave her right arm behind. She wouldn't go without the child, and he wouldn't go without her, so they were stuck at an impasse.

"Mom, we have to give Vicki to her."

Sophie stepped from the edge of the woods, the baby cradled on her shoulder. The girl was barefoot, dressed only in a thin cotton nightgown.

"Sophie!" Phoenix cried. "What are you doing here?"

"I saw you take the bow and arrow from under the bed and I wanted to know what you were doing." She moved closer. "You always said you would give Vicki back to Freedom if she came for her," she said. "If Hannah is her sister, she's the next best thing."

Phoenix touched her daughter's cheek, then laid her other hand on the baby's back.

"You always said children belonged with family," Sophie said.

"I did, didn't I?" She turned back to Hannah. "You're not lying to me, are you?"

"Everything I've told you is the truth," Hannah said.

Except that she and Walt weren't really husband and wife, he thought, but what bearing did that have on any of this?

Phoenix handed the bow and arrow to Walt, then took the sleeping infant from Sophie and put her in Hannah's arms.

Sophie slipped the diaper bag onto Hannah's shoulder. "Some of her things are in here, including some bottles of formula and some diapers."

"Thanks," Hannah said, and patted the girl's hand.

"Take good care of her," Phoenix whispered.

"I will," Hannah said. "And thank you—for being my sister's friend, for taking care of her baby and for helping me. You're a good woman, Phoenix."

She said nothing, but took Sophie's hand and turned away. "I'll light a candle for you," she said.

"Wait!" Hannah called.

Phoenix looked back over her shoulder.

"You should come with us," Hannah said.

"No." Phoenix took a step back. "This is my home. This is where I belong."

"But what if someone tries to hurt you?" Hannah asked. "Because you helped us?"

Phoenix smiled. "I'm sure that won't happen. We're safer here than we would be anywhere else."

Walt could see Hannah didn't believe that, but he doubted she would ever convince the older woman she was in danger. Phoenix still believed in the Prophet, despite everything that had happened. "We'll stay in touch," Hannah said. "We'll make sure you're all right." She would ask the Rangers to keep an eye on mother and daughter—to make sure no harm came to them.

WALT SHOULDERED THE crude bow and arrow, then took Hannah's hand. "Come on," he said. "We'd better go."

"I can't wait to get out of here," she said, hurrying along beside him.

"We have to stop by Kiram's place first," he said.

She balked. "Why do we have to go there?"

"I have to get my shoes—and my gun."

She glanced down at his bare feet. "Are you sure it's worth the risk?"

"We won't let him see us. You can hide somewhere nearby while I go inside."

She tucked the blankets more securely around the baby. "Let's get it over with, then."

They found a spot in the woods away from the camp but close enough to give them a view of Kiram's shack. People were beginning to emerge from some of the other trailers and tents, but there was no sign of life around the makeshift dwelling. Walt was beginning to wonder if they had missed the bearded man. "Maybe I should see if the place is empty," he said.

"No." Hannah's fingers dug into his arm. When he turned to look at her, she fixed him with a fierce gaze. "I almost lost you to that bully once," she said. "I don't want to risk it again."

Her words made him feel a little unsteady, as if reeling from a punch. He wanted to demand she explain what she meant, but now didn't seem the right time. Instead, he covered her hand with his own and nodded. "All right. We'll wait a little longer."

Just as he turned back to the shack, the door opened and Kiram emerged. As usual, he wore the knife at his waist. He looked around him, then headed away, toward the center of the camp, where other Family members were gathering for breakfast.

As soon as he was out of sight, Walt rushed forward. He took cover around the side of the shack for a moment, catching his breath. No one shouted or gave any other sign they had seen him. Quickly, he moved to the door and slipped inside.

He went first to the rafter where he had hidden the gun, and breathed a sigh of relief when he found it still there. He checked that the weapon was still loaded, then tucked it into the waistband of his jeans. His shoes were also where he had left them. He put them on, then looked around to see if he had missed anything. Moments later, he rejoined Hannah. "Let's get the bike and get out of here," he said.

"Do you think it's safe to take the baby on the motorcycle?" she asked as they made their way along the creek toward the parking area.

"It's not the safest choice," he said. "But I don't think we have any other option."

"No. I don't suppose we do."

On the way to the parking area, he dumped the bow and arrows into the brush. "I appreciate Phoenix looking out for you," he said. "But I'm more comfortable with my service weapon than those."

"I guess a gun would be more reliable," Hannah said. "Though I hope it doesn't come to that."

They emerged on the edge of the gravel parking area. As usual, the area was empty. They kept to cover until they came to the place where Walt had left the bike, camouflaged with branches. He peered into the thick underbrush and saw a few loose branches on the ground, but no bike.

"I don't see it," Hannah said.

He swore under his breath and kicked at the dirt, where the imprint of the motorcycle's tires clearly showed. "It was here," he said. "Someone took it."

"Metwater wanted it," she said. "He must have hidden it away somewhere."

"That would be my guess." Add theft to his list of charges against the so-called prophet.

"What are we going to do?" she asked.

"We start walking."

"That's right. You can turn around and walk back into camp." The underbrush behind them moved and

Kiram emerged. Though Kiram still wore his knife, he aimed a pistol at Walt. “Start walking,” he said. “Or I’ll take a great deal of pleasure in shooting you.”

Chapter Fifteen

Walt stepped in front of Hannah and the baby. He had to give them a chance to get away. Metwater wanted Hannah, but Kiram hated Walt, and Walt could use that fact to his advantage. "What's with the gun?" he asked. "I thought you were a peace-loving guy focused on spiritual matters."

"Shut up and start walking." Kiram motioned with the gun toward camp. The way he was waving the weapon around made Walt think he hadn't handled guns a lot—or at least he hadn't been trained to handle them safely. Which made him more dangerous, but less likely to be a really good shot.

Walt reached back and took Hannah's hand. "We'll come quietly," he lied. "Just allow us one more kiss before you tear us apart again." Before Kiram could respond, he pulled Hannah close and kissed her soundly on the mouth. She stiffened, then melted into his arms. He would have liked to prolong the moment, to savor the feel of her lips on his. But they didn't have a moment to lose. With his back partially shielding her from view, he moved his mouth to her ear.

"When I give the word, run," he said. "I'll be with you as soon as I can."

"Yes," she whispered.

He released her and turned to face Kiram once more. "Get going!" the bearded man shouted.

"I'm going." He took two steps toward the other man, then launched himself at Kiram's legs, sending him flying. "Run!" he shouted, and prayed that Hannah wouldn't hesitate to flee.

Kiram grunted as he landed hard on his back, but he kept hold of the gun. By the time he sat up, Walt had drawn his own weapon. Kiram fired, but the shot went wild. He rolled to the side as Walt fired, so that the bullet struck him in the shoulder, instead of the chest. Kiram's eyes widened in shock. He dropped his weapon and clutched at his shoulder, where blood blossomed, seeping through his fingers.

Walt kicked Kiram's gun away as loud voices approached. The others in the camp must have heard the shots. "Help!" Kiram shouted. "He's getting away!"

Walt didn't wait to hear more. He took off in the direction Hannah had fled. He had run several hundred yards, away from the road and the camp, when he heard her call his name. "Walt! Over here!"

He found her huddled in a thick growth of scrub oak, the baby clutched to her chest. "Are you all right?" she asked, her expression pale and stressed.

"I'm okay." He crouched in front of her. He needed to touch her, to reassure himself that she really was okay. He smoothed her hair back from her face. "What about you?"

"I'm okay." She put one hand to his cheek. "I heard gunshots and I was so worried."

"Kiram fired on me, and I shot him."

"Is he dead?"

"No. I hit him in the shoulder, but he should recover."

"As long as you're safe." She pulled his mouth down to hers and kissed him hard, as if trying to drive away all fear and doubt. He gripped her shoulders and returned the kiss, not holding back any of the emotion he felt. He didn't care that this thing between them was impractical and poorly timed and likely doomed—he was going to enjoy it now, for whatever time together they had.

Voices rose in the direction of camp and he pulled away. "We'd better go," he said. "The more distance we can put between us and Metwater's followers, the better."

He stood and helped her to her feet. The baby began to cry. "I need to change her diaper," Hannah said.

"Hurry." He looked over his shoulder, the way they had come. Though he couldn't see anyone headed toward them, Metwater's enforcers were bound to pursue them as soon as they got the story from Kiram.

When he turned back to Hannah, she had laid the baby out on the blanket and removed the old diaper, which she placed in a plastic bag and stuffed in the diaper bag. "I guess we can't count on help from anyone in camp," she said.

"Some of them, like Phoenix, might want to help, but I think Metwater has most of them firmly under his thumb. I don't think we can risk it."

She nodded and fastened the new diaper around the baby, who kicked her feet and babbled. Walt smiled and held out his finger for her to grip. "You're going to be a great mom," he said.

She stared at him. "Do you really think so?"

Clearly, his answer mattered to her. He patted her shoulder. "You already love her, and that's what's most important."

Nodding, she rewrapped the blanket and zipped shut the diaper bag. "What do we do next?"

"We head for Ranger headquarters." He stood and helped her to her feet. "We'll have to travel cross-country. Metwater's people are likely to be looking for us along the roads."

They set out, trying to stay in cover as much as possible, alert to any sounds of pursuit, which didn't come. The sun climbed overhead, the day already hot. Walt wished he had thought to bring water. The creek that ran alongside Metwater's camp was the only water source he knew of around here and they couldn't risk detouring back that way. But it should only take them a few hours to reach the main road. From there they might be able to catch a ride to Ranger headquarters or into Montrose. They could call for help from there.

They paralleled the road leading away from the camp, but the going was slow, the ground rocky and uneven. Every hundred yards or so they had to detour around a pile of boulders or a dry wash or an expanse of cactus. All signs of the previous night's rain had vanished, the ground dry as powder beneath their feet, the air heavy with the scent of sagebrush and cedar.

Though they kept out of sight of the road, the rumble of passing traffic reached them, and dust clouds from the passing cars rose up in the air. "Do you think it's Family members looking for us?" she asked.

"I can't think who else it would be." Walt followed yet another dust plume with his eyes. "These roads normally get hardly any traffic."

"Maybe one of the Rangers will stop by the camp and someone will tell them we're gone," she said.

"We should have headed toward the grave site," he said. "The forensics team might still be working there. I don't know why I didn't think of that before."

"It was too close to camp," she said. "It's probably one of the first places Metwater will look. And you don't even know if anyone is still there."

"No." He wasn't even sure he could find the grave

site now—not without returning to the camp as his starting point, and that was far too risky.

They had walked only an hour or so when he noticed Hannah limping. "What's wrong?" he asked, stopping. "Are you hurt?"

She grimaced. "Blister."

"Let me take the baby." He held his arms out and after a moment's hesitation, she handed the child over.

He settled the infant into the crook of his arm, a warm weight. She smiled up at him and he smiled back, enchanted.

"She's just like her mother," Hannah said. "Emily could always charm any man."

"You're pretty charming yourself," Walt said.

"Ha! I'm a lot of things, but charming is not one of them."

"All right, what about—alluring."

Pink warmed her cheeks, but she said nothing, merely set out walking again.

He caught up with her. "Why does that catch you so off guard?" he asked. "Me saying you're alluring?"

"Because I'm not," she said.

"You can't pretend you don't know I'm attracted to you. And you're attracted to me."

"I don't want to be."

He recognized truth when he heard it. "I get that, but I don't understand why."

She glanced at him, then went back to focusing on the ground. "You don't have to understand."

"But I want to."

She said nothing, only quickened her pace. He lengthened his stride to keep up with her. "When I first met you, I thought I had you figured out," he said. "I saw a smart career woman, someone used to being in charge. You became the guardian of your dead sister's baby and you threw yourself into preparing for motherhood the way you would any other project."

She said nothing, so he kept talking, refusing to let her silence shut him out. "You had probably researched all the best products and techniques, maybe arranged for child care, found a pediatrician, furnished a nursery. You had a plan for what things would be like when you got back to Texas."

"Is there something wrong with that?" she asked.

"Nothing. Except then we started working together and these feelings grew between us and I'm not a part of your plan."

"I can't be in a relationship right now."

"Why not? You don't think you can love that baby and me at the same time? People do it every day."

"I'm not every person," she said.

"No, and that's why I love you." He grabbed her hand, stopping her and turning her to him. He waited for her to rebel, to tell him he couldn't possibly love her, she didn't love him, they lived in different states, the whole situation was impossible…

Instead, she stared at him, eyes wide and shimmering with tears. "You can't love me," she said.

"Why not?"

"Because you don't know me. You don't know the awful things I've done."

"Awful things? What awful things?" A chill crept into his chest as he studied her grave expression and read the mixture of pain and fear in her eyes. Had he misjudged her so badly?

Tears were streaming down her face now. She turned away, hugging her arms across her body. Walt shifted the baby to his other arm and moved up behind her, caressing her shoulders. "I can't believe you've ever done anything so awful it would change the way I feel about you," he said.

"Emily knew. It was one of the reasons why she ran away."

"But she gave you her baby. That must mean she forgave you."

She nodded. "Yes. Yes, I think she forgave me."

"Tell me," he said. "You need to tell me or we'll both always wonder what would have happened if you had."

She sniffed, but a fresh wave of sobs shook her. He handed her his handkerchief and waited while she dabbed at her eyes and blew her nose. "I had a baby once," she said.

He blinked. He had never expected this. She had a baby? When? With whom? But none of those questions spoke to the pain in her eyes. "What happened?" he asked.

"I was nineteen. I had just started college and I had a...a fling. Nothing serious. When I got pregnant the guy freaked out. We both agreed we couldn't raise a child, so I decided to give the baby up for adoption."

"I'm sure that wasn't an easy decision. But it doesn't make you a bad person. You gave someone else who badly wanted to be a parent the chance to do so."

"It was the hardest decision I ever made." She drew in a ragged breath. "I chose an open adoption, because I wanted to know what happened to my child. Everything went well. The couple was very nice. Then, when she was three months old, little Madison died."

Another sob shook her. He gathered her close and held her tight. "I'm so sorry," he whispered, stroking her hair.

"They said it was crib death—just something that happens sometimes. But I can't help thinking, if I had been there, I could have kept her safe. If I had taken care of my own child, that wouldn't have happened."

"You can't know that," he said. "Terrible things happen sometimes, for no reason."

"I know. That's what the counselors I saw said, too. But it's haunted me. It made me believe I didn't deserve to be happy. I threw myself into my work because that was something I could control—something that didn't depend on emotion and chance. And then Emily gave me this second chance to be a mother." She smiled down at Joy, who lay sleeping in his arms.

"You're going to be a great mom to her," Walt said. "I believe that."

"But I can't take any chances," she said. "I can't let myself be distracted. Not even by you."

He could argue that he wouldn't be a distraction—that he could help her with the baby and everything would be all right. But he wasn't the one whose baby had died. He wasn't the one who was suffering.

And he couldn't think of any argument that would change her mind. Only time and experience could do that. She stepped away from him and he let her go. "Just know you're not alone," he said. "I will be there for you if you need me."

Her expression grew less bleak. "Thank you," she said. "That means a lot."

"Thank you for trusting me with your story," he said. "Hearing it doesn't change how I feel about you. If anything, it makes me admire you all the more."

"How can you say that?"

"You suffered something terrible. But you didn't let it defeat you. You came out the other side. I've seen the kind of courage you have and now I know some of what's behind it."

She studied his face, as if searching for something there. "I never met anyone like you," she said.

"I hope that's a good thing."

The baby woke and began to cry. Hannah took the child from him. "She's probably hungry," she said. "We should stop and feed her."

He looked around, then led the way to the meager shade of a stunted pinyon. Hannah settled herself against the trunk and pulled out a bottle of formula for the baby. Walt sat beside her and tried not to think about how thirsty he was.

A loud vehicle passed on the road a quarter mile distant, the rumble of an exhaust system with a hole in it echoing across the empty landscape. "Why are they pursuing us like this?" Hannah asked.

"Because Metwater knows we'll go to the police," Walt said. "We'll tell them about him kidnapping you and assaulting me, stealing my motorcycle, lying about your sister—all the things he's done. That will lead to more digging into his activities. My guess is that an investigation will turn up more crimes—things he doesn't want us finding out."

"He's built a little kingdom out here and he thinks he can control everyone in it," Hannah said. "He thought he was safe."

"He wasn't able to control us," Walt said. "And that's made him angry—and dangerous."

"How much longer before we reach somewhere safe?" she asked. She stowed the bottle and zipped up the diaper bag, then rested the baby on her shoulder and patted her back. She looked so comfortable and natural with the infant—he started to point this out, but then thought better of bringing up what was obviously a painful topic.

"We've only got another hour or two to walk and we should be able to flag down a car," he said. "Once we're in the park, there will be more tourist traffic. Someone will help us."

"I hope so." She held up her hand and he pulled her to her feet and they set out walking again.

They hadn't gone far when they came to a deep gash in the landscape—a narrow, rocky ravine. Walt peered into the shadowy, brush-choked canyon. "It's too steep to climb down into and out again," he said. "Especially with the baby."

Hannah shielded her eyes and peered down the length of the ravine. "It looks as if it goes on for miles."

"We'll have to walk up to the road. There's a culvert and a bridge there."

Hannah drew back. "Is that safe?"

"We can hear and see cars approaching from a long way off," he said. "We'll hide until we're sure the coast is clear, then make a dash for it."

They turned and followed the ravine up toward the road. As they drew closer, the rumble of an approaching vehicle sent them diving for cover behind an outcropping of pocked rock. Heat radiated from the scarred red granite, but the ground on its shady side still gave off a damp coolness.

Walt peered over the top of the boulder and

watched a faded brown Jeep move slowly past. A bearded man sat behind the wheel; Walt was sure it was Kiram, but was that even possible, considering how recently he had been wounded?

When the vehicle had passed, they moved forward again. The bridge over the ravine was a plank affair one lane wide, laid over a rusting metal culvert. No railings separated traffic from the chasm below, and only a single orange reflector on a post marked the beginning of the bridge.

"It didn't seem this narrow when we were on the motorcycle," Hannah said.

"All we have to do is walk across it and we can move away from the road again." Walt held out his hand and she took it.

Their feet made a hollow sound on the wood planks, but the bridge was solid underfoot, and only about twenty feet across. Halfway across, the baby began to fuss and squirm. Hannah stopped and shifted her. "Her diaper's soaking," she said, feeling around one chubby leg. "No wonder, considering the way she sucked down that bottle."

"You can change her in another couple of minutes," Walt said. Standing out here in the middle of the bridge felt too vulnerable. The hair rose on the back of his neck, and he couldn't shake the feeling they were being watched. A hot wind ruffled his hair and he squinted across the prairie, his unease growing.

"What was that noise?" Hannah looked up from tending the baby.

Walt didn't have to ask "what noise?" He heard it, too—the low rumble of an engine turning over. He pivoted toward the sound, and saw what he hadn't noticed before—an old wooden corral, the boards forming the sides almost obscured by several decades' growth of sagebrush and prickly pear cactus. The corral made the perfect hiding place for someone in a vehicle to park and watch the bridge and wait.

The driver wasn't waiting anymore. His vehicle—a faded brown Jeep—shot out from the screen of boards and brush, headed straight for the bridge, and Walt and Hannah standing in the middle of it.

Chapter Sixteen

Hannah froze, transfixed by the sight of the Jeep barreling toward them. She was like someone in a dream, wanting to move but unable to do so.

"Climb down!" Walt tugged on her arm. "Over the side. Into the culvert." He pulled the infant from her and dragged her toward the edge of the bridge. He dropped to his stomach and pulled her down alongside him. "Go!" he urged.

She swung her legs over the side, clinging to the edge of the bridge, the boards shaking as the Jeep hit the bridge, the roar of the engine filling her ears. The baby clutched to his chest, Walt swung down beside her and dropped to the ground. She released her hold on the bridge as the Jeep thundered over them.

She hit the ground hard, the breath jolted out of her, but managed to roll into the culvert. Walt helped her to her feet and shoved the baby into her arms. "Get behind me," he said, drawing his gun and moving into the shadows.

Tires skidded on gravel as the Jeep braked to a halt.

Car doors slammed and footsteps crunched. Hannah shrank into the deepest shadows, heart thudding so hard in her chest she had trouble drawing breath. Walt guided her into the middle of the tunnel formed by the culvert, into a corner formed by wooden bracing. He settled her into this hiding place, then turned, his back to her, shielding her with his body. She stared over his shoulder toward the opening at the end of the culvert, a circle of bright light like a spotlight, blinding in its intensity.

Each footstep overhead seemed to echo through the tunnel. Obviously, their pursuers were making no attempt at stealth. The movement above stopped. "We know you're in there, Walter!" Kiram shouted. "Come on out and we'll go easy on you."

Walt remained silent, still as a cornered stag—or a waiting lion.

Two heavy thuds signaled that their two pursuers had dropped into the ravine—one on either side of the culvert. Hannah stiffened. They were trapped now, caught between the two.

Walt reached back and squeezed her hand. The gesture shouldn't have calmed her, but somehow it did. Without uttering a word, he was letting her know he had a plan. She had to trust him.

She took a deep breath and squeezed back. *I trust you.*

A shadow darkened the opening to the tunnel—

the silhouette of a tall, muscular man. "You can't escape now," Kiram said. "We've got you cornered."

He raised his right arm, and Hannah recognized the silhouette of a gun before it melted into the shadow of his body. But he was aiming it at the opposite side of the tunnel from where they were standing. He hadn't yet seen them. They were hidden in the deepest, darkest recesses of the tunnel, and his eyes, attuned to the brightness outside, hadn't been able to make them out. The man at the other end of the tunnel wouldn't be able to see them either, especially since the wooden support completely blocked them from his view.

Kiram took a step into the tunnel. Walt would have a clear shot at him now. Didn't Kiram realize this? Or was he so sure of his own superior position that he wasn't thinking? But would Walt fire? As soon as he did so, he would give away their position to the other man.

"It's too late to save yourself," Kiram said. "I promised to kill you and I will. But you can save the woman. The Prophet wants her and the baby safe and alive. Give yourself up now and I promise to take them to him. Try to take me and…well, I can't help it if they get caught in the cross fire, can I?" He took another step toward them.

The shot was a loud, echoing explosion in the metal culvert. Hannah choked back a scream and sank to her knees, her body arched over the baby, who began to wail. A second shot followed the first, then two more in rapid succession. Head down, eyes squeezed tightly shut, Hannah couldn't tell where they came from.

Her ears rang, and the smell of gunpowder stung her nose, but even half-deaf, the scuffle of retreating footsteps was clear. Opening her eyes, she turned to see Walt racing toward the far end of the tunnel. Before he had reached the end, an engine roared to life overhead, and tires skidded as the Jeep raced away.

Walt returned to her, the gun still in his hand. "Are you all right?" he asked.

"Yes." She started to rise, and he bent to help her. "What happened?" she asked.

"I'm going to check on Kiram," he said, and left before she could say more. Too shaken to move, she leaned back against the support and held her breath as he moved slowly toward the slumped figure at the tunnel opening.

She knew Kiram was dead by the heavy, sack-of-cement way his body rolled over when Walt nudged it. Walt knelt and put a hand to the bearded man's neck, then eased the gun from his grip and tucked it into his belt. He took something else from the body, then returned to her side.

"Here." He pressed something heavy into her hand. "He was wearing this on his belt."

She realized she was holding a water bottle, and hurried to twist off the cap and drink. The cool, sweet water flowed over her tongue and tears stung her eyes at the sheer pleasure of it. She forced herself to hold back from drinking it all and passed it to him.

"The other man got away," she said, when Walt had finished drinking and re-capped the bottle.

"Yes. He'll tell the others we're in this area. We need to move quickly."

"Why did he come after us?" she asked. "I thought you shot him back at the camp."

"I wounded him, but it obviously wasn't enough to stop him. His shoulder was bandaged, but my guess is he hated me enough that he was determined to find me. That kind of emotion can lead people to do incredible things."

"But he didn't stop us," she said. "He won't stop us."

"No, he won't." He started to lead the way out of the culvert, but she took hold of his arm, turning him toward her.

"What—?" She cut off the question, her lips on his, her body pressed against him. All the fear and anxiety and the giddy relief of simply being alive and with him at this moment coalesced in that kiss. All the passion she felt for him but was afraid to put into words found expression in the melding of her body to his.

He wrapped his arms around her, crushing her to him. There was no hiding her body's response to him, or his to her. Heat and hunger and need washed over her like a wave, and she moaned softly as he caressed the side of her breast and lowered his mouth to nibble the soft underside of her jaw. Every kiss, every caress, reached past the barriers she had erected long ago and touched some vulnerable part of her deep inside, coaxing her to let go a little bit more, to surrender. To trust.

He rested his forehead against hers, his breathing ragged, his voice rough. "This isn't the best time for this," he said.

"I know." She rested her palms against his chest. "We have to go. I just… I wanted you to know how I felt."

"I got the message, loud and clear." He wrapped both hands around her wrists and kissed the tips of her fingers, a gesture that set her heart to fluttering wildly.

Then he released her, and she wanted to cry out, but instead bit her lip and bent to pick up the baby, who smiled up at her with such an expression of happiness that tears stung her eyes. Talk about an emotional roller-coaster ride! The last thirty minutes had taken her through almost every feeling imaginable.

They moved out of the tunnel, the light momentarily blinding them after so much time in the shadows. Joy wailed, and Hannah rearranged the blanket to shade her face. "We'll stick to the ravine," Walt said. "It'll be rough going, but we'll be out of sight of the road."

Navigating the ravine was akin to negotiating an

obstacle course. Uprooted trees, boulders the size of furniture, loose gravel and tangles of thorny vines necessitated frequent detours and stumbles. After a short distance Walt took the baby so that Hannah had both hands free to steady herself as she climbed up boulders and teetered along downed tree trunks. She stumbled often, scraping her hands and muddying her skirt. But she plowed doggedly on. As difficult as this was, at least they weren't out in the open, where anyone looking for them might easily spot them.

They had been walking less than an hour—and covered maybe half a mile—when the roar of approaching vehicles made them freeze in midstride. "It sounds like at least two of them," Walt said.

"Are they on the road?" Hannah asked, straining her ears.

As if to answer her question, the engine sounds faded, followed by crunching gravel, then the engines revved with a different pitch than before. "They turned off the road," Walt said. "They're headed this way."

He turned and continued moving up the ravine. "What are we going to do?" she asked, hurrying after him.

"As long as they stay in the vehicles, they can't see us down here," Walt said. He reached out a hand to pull her up over a large section of dead tree that was wedged across the ravine. "As long as they don't stop and get out, they're just wasting gas racing around up there."

"How did they find us so quickly?" she asked.

"They might have radios."

The engine noises faded again, and car doors slammed. Hannah looked up, and wished she knew what was going on up there.

"We'd better find a place to hide," Walt said.

They moved farther down the ravine, losing their footing often on the rough ground, but pressing on. The ravine forked and Walt led her down the narrower branch, which was scarcely wide enough for them to walk side by side. This channel was more deeply eroded, but less clogged with debris, though tree roots reached out from the bank like bony fingers, snagging at their clothing and hair.

"In here." Walt indicated a place where the bank was undercut behind a snarl of tree roots, forming a recess. Hannah balked, staring at what was really a mud-lined hole in the ground. It looked like the perfect home for spiders, snakes and who knew what else.

"Come on," Walt urged. "We have to hide before they decide to search here."

He was right, and there was no sense being squeamish. She followed him into the niche. He handed her the baby, then pulled the tree roots and a couple of loose branches to cover their entrance.

Sunlight filtered through the network of limbs and

branches that formed one wall of their shelter, dappling their faces and making the niche a little less threatening. Hannah settled back into an almost-cozy spot and took out a fresh diaper and a packet of wipes. At least she could make Joy more comfortable. She stashed the dirty diaper in a plastic bag and stuffed it into the diaper bag, which she used as a kind of pillow at her back.

"Here." Walt handed her a protein bar. "Dinner."

"Thanks. You think of everything."

"Yeah. I really know how to show a woman a good time." He unwrapped a bar for himself. "Take this out-of-the-way bistro. You can't imagine how exclusive this place is."

"And it's so romantic." She laughed, and he grinned and rested his hand on her knee. "Anyplace with you seems romantic to me."

She debated kissing him again, but the narrow confines of their hideaway—not to mention the baby on her lap—made that difficult. So she settled for lacing her fingers in his and soaking in the feeling of contentment that filled her. She was dirty, hungry, thirsty and exhausted, terrified of the killers who hunted them, and confused about what lay ahead for her and Joy. But all of those worries and fears faded into the background here beside Walt.

They shared the last of the water, munching in companionable silence while straining their ears for any sound from the searchers overhead. "It doesn't sound as if they've come this way," Walt said after a while. "They probably didn't expect us to get this far. They might even suspect we went another direction."

He shifted to turn toward her. "What happened last night?" he asked. "When Metwater took you to his RV?" Tension radiated from him, as if he was bracing for bad news.

"Nothing, really," she said. "He seemed to think I ought to be flattered that I'd been singled out for attention from the great and mighty Prophet." She made a face. "The guy has an ego bigger than his biceps."

"So he didn't try to force himself on you?"

"He intended to keep me prisoner until I came around to his way of thinking." She sighed. "I think that's what he did with Emily. At least, Phoenix told me he had moved her in with him a week or so before she died. Taking her with him to Denver was a special privilege—maybe an attempt to persuade her to give in to his demands. I think the stress of the whole ordeal, and being without her baby, brought on her asthma attack. Plus, Phoenix told me she had run out of her inhaler prescription."

"It would be tough to prove murder, though if what you say is true, he could have definitely contributed to her death."

"I know. But then, why lie and say she had run away instead of telling people she had died?"

"Because he didn't want to upset the rest of his followers?" He put his arm around her. "We may never know. Though when I bring in Metwater, I intend to ask him."

She settled against him, her head on his shoulder. "Knowing you care means a lot."

He kissed the top of her head. "I do care."

Yes. And she cared for him. But if caring were enough, her baby never would have died. She had made a mistake then, trying to do the right thing. She couldn't afford to make another mistake.

DESPITE THE DISCOMFORT of her surroundings and the lingering fear for their safety, the sleepless night in Metwater's RV, coupled with the physical hardship of fleeing across the wilderness, overcame Hannah's attempts to stay awake, and she sank into a deep slumber.

She woke to Joy's cries the next morning, sunlight streaking down from above. Next to her, Walt stirred. "I'm going to go up and check things out," he said. "See if it's safe for us to move on."

He moved out of their shelter, and she took advantage of his absence to spread out the contents of the diaper bag and organize them. She had one more bottle of formula, which she would feed Joy this morning—and only two more diapers. No more water or food for her and Walt. But surely this morning they would reach safety. They couldn't be that far from the highway after they had walked so much yesterday.

A shower of dirt signaled Walt's return. "Everything's quiet up here," he said. "I think it's safe to go."

"Let me change Joy," she said. "She can have her last bottle while we're walking."

"I don't suppose you've stashed any coffee in there," he said, eyeing the diaper bag.

"I wish. I guess all the coffee shops up there are closed?"

"Every one of them." He waited while she finished diapering the baby, then reached down to help them out of their hiding place.

She groaned as she put weight on her cramped limbs. "I think every bone in my body hurts," she said.

"We'll have to complain to management about the mattresses in this place," Walt said.

They climbed out of the ravine and she paused at the top to stretch and breathe in the fresh, clean air, which smelled of sage and wildflowers. After spending so much time out here, she would never look at the wilderness as barren again. "Which way do we go?" she asked.

Walt turned in a slow circle, taking in the surrounding landscape. The land was gently rolling, and devoid of any sign of human habitation. Only scrubby prairie and the occasional rock uplift defined the empty expanse. Hannah had hoped to see a road, but no such luck. "Does anything look familiar to you?" he asked.

"Everything out here looks the same to me," she said.

"Me, too."

His grim expression alarmed her. “Are you saying we’re lost?”

“I’m saying I’m not sure which way we should go to find the road.”

She turned to look behind them, at the ravine they had just climbed out of. “Can’t we just follow this back to the BLM road, then parallel that to the highway?” she asked. As much as she hated the thought of backtracking, it would be better than wandering aimlessly in the middle of nowhere.

“We could. If we knew which ravine to follow.” He indicated the network of half a dozen similar ditches that spread out in every direction.

“I don’t remember those,” she said. “When we were down in there, there was only one way to go, at least, after we took the fork off the main channel.”

“There were other forks,” he said. “Now I’m not sure which one we should take.”

She looked down into the chasm again. The thought of repeating the torturous crawl of the day before made her want to sink to her knees and weep. But she was stronger than that. “Do you know which direction the road was from Metwater’s camp?” she asked.

“East,” he said.

“The sun rises in the east, so we can walk that direction,” she said.

“Except we don’t know where we are in relationship to Metwater’s camp,” he said.

"So you're saying we're lost."

He squinted up at the sky. "Yeah. I guess I'm saying we're lost."

The words seemed to bounce up against her brain, refusing to sink in. After all they had been through, this couldn't really be happening. "You work out here," she said. "Don't you have some idea of where we are?"

"I've only been on the job two months," he said. "And it's a lot of territory. It would take years—decades—for any one person to know it all."

"So what are we going to do?" She hated that they were in this situation—and she hated that she was looking to him for answers. She wasn't the kind of person who depended on other people. She was used to solving her own problems. But this wasn't a chemical formulation that needed tweaking or a budget item she needed to finesse. She had nothing to draw on to get them out of this jam.

"Right now, I think we've got an even bigger problem to worry about," Walt said.

"What are you talking about?" What could be bigger than being lost in the middle of nowhere?

"If I'm not mistaken, we've got a prairie fire headed this way."

She turned to follow his gaze and gaped at the line of leaping orange flames that filled the horizon.

Chapter Seventeen

Walt stared at the line of flames inching toward them, the lessons from a wildland firefighting course he had taken as part of his training repeating in his head. The wind was pushing the fire in this direction, and there was nothing to stop it, and plenty of dry tinder to feed it. Firefighters carried flameproof shelters which—sometimes—could save their lives if they were overtaken by an out-of-control burn, but he and Hannah didn't have anything like that.

He took hold of her arm. "We have to get back into the ravine," he said. "If we're lucky, it will divert the flames, or they'll pass over it."

She didn't hesitate or argue, merely wrapped the baby more securely and started half climbing, half sliding into the ditch they had only recently climbed out of. "Try to find the cave where we spent the night!" he shouted after her. Already the roar of the fire was growing louder, like a jet engine revving for flight. The wind blowing toward them carried the scent of burning wood—like the world's largest campfire.

He caught up with her at the bottom of the ravine and together they scrambled over boulders and branches, watching for the opening to the undercut that had sheltered them last night.

"There!" Hannah pointed to the place where they had pushed aside a knot of tree roots as they had exited their shelter.

"Hurry!" He took the baby from her and started up the slope. The fire was almost upon them, a hot, shrieking turbulence created by the flames sending debris flying, branches and even whole trees exploding into flames like hand grenades going off as the sap superheated inside the bark.

He shoved the baby, who was crying now, into the mud-lined shelter, then reached back to haul Hannah up by both arms. He pushed her into the opening, then crawled in after her, shielding both her and the child with his body, his back to the world above that was already being consumed by flames.

Hannah crouched over the infant, whose wails rose over even the sound of the inferno, a siren song that seemed to intensify his own fear and anxiety. He wrapped his arms around Hannah and buried his face against her neck, breathing in deeply of her sweet scent, trying to block the acrid stench of smoke. She gripped his arm, fingers digging into his flesh. The roar of the flames was even louder now—he winced as the heat intensified, searing his back. It was growing harder to breathe, and the baby's wails silenced. He slid one hand beneath Hannah's to touch the child, reassured that she was still breathing.

Hannah coughed, and he held her, then gave in to spasms of his own. But as the pain in his chest eased, he opened his eyes and realized the roaring of the blaze had faded, and light was once more seeping into their shelter. The heat had lessened, as well. Hannah turned her head and her eyes met his. "Is it over?" she asked.

He eased back a little, and then a little more, until he was able to stick his head out to survey the ravine. Smoke curled from a smoldering tree branch and white ash scarred the rocks around it, but the fire hadn't descended to the bottom of the ravine. He retreated into the undercut once more. "Let's wait a few minutes for things to cool off a bit, but I think we're okay," he said. "How's Joy?"

"She's fine." She cradled the infant to her, tears streaming down her face. "I was so scared, but thanks to you, we're all okay."

"I didn't do anything," he said. "And for what it's worth, I was terrified, too."

She wrapped her arms around him. "I might have made it without you, but I'm glad I didn't have to try," she said.

They waited half an hour, then climbed out of the ravine, emerging streaked with soot and ash to a landscape filled with the blackened skeletons of trees and exploded rock. Smoke curled from the ground, and they walked carefully, trying to avoid hot spots. Walt moved in front of Hannah to break the trail, and she gasped.

He glanced over his shoulder at her. “What’s wrong?”

“Your back!” She pointed, then covered her mouth with her hand. “It’s burned.”

He hadn’t noticed anything until that moment, but when he reached around and felt along his ribs he winced at the sudden, searing pain. “Your shirt is almost burned away,” she said. “You let that happen and you never said a thing.”

“I had other things on my mind.” He faced forward again. “It doesn’t matter. We have to get out of here.”

“But where are we going?” she asked.

“Away from the fire.”

A droning sound overhead made them both look up. When Walt recognized the helicopter, he raised both hands to wave, ignoring the pain in his shoulders as he did so. Hannah took the blanket from around the baby and waved it also. The chopper dipped lower, and they could clearly see the pilot. He circled them, and then slowly descended to a spot about two hundred yards away.

By the time Walt and Hannah reached the helicopter, the pilot had shut down the engine and climbed out to meet them. "What are you two doing out here?" he asked.

"It's a long story," Walt said. "I'm Agent Walt Riley with the Ranger Brigade. Can you take us to Ranger headquarters?"

"Whoever you are, you need to get out of here. Climb in." The pilot walked around to the door of the chopper. "I'll radio this in once we're airborne. Headquarters is never going to believe this."

"I DON'T BELIEVE THIS." Commander Graham Ellison frowned as an EMT bandaged Walt's blistered back. "When Metwater's people told us you and Hannah had left, we suspected something was up, but not that you'd been trapped in that wildfire."

"Which the fire investigators now say was deliberately set." Carmen joined the group clustered around Walt, Hannah and the baby.

"When Metwater's goons didn't succeed in tracking us down yesterday, he probably thought the fire would be a good way to finish us off." Walt winced as the EMT tightened the bandage.

"That's crazy." Hannah looked up from feeding the baby. "They could have burned down their own camp."

"They were probably counting on the road and the creek to serve as a firebreak," Marco said. "And the prevailing winds were in their favor."

"Metwater is already claiming he knows nothing about anything," Graham said. "And he's telling anyone who will listen that you murdered Alan Saddler—aka Kiram—in cold blood."

"He was trying to kill us!" Hannah stood, unable to rein in her outrage.

"I'm sure the investigation will prove that," Graham said. He turned to Walt. "Until that plays out, you're probably going to take a beating in the press. Metwater has his lawyers working overtime, filing charges."

"But he'll have to submit to the paternity test the court ordered, right?" Hannah asked. Soon after they had arrived at Ranger headquarters, she had learned the court order for the DNA test to determine the baby's identity had come through.

"He will," Graham said. "We won't let him off the hook on that."

The EMT pressed the final bandage in place, then stepped back. "You need to have a doctor check that out ASAP, but I'm guessing you're going to need a couple of weeks off to heal," he said.

"Good idea," Graham said. "You lie low and let us handle Metwater."

"He assaulted me, kidnapped Hannah and he stole my bike," Walt said.

"I've got your bike in my garage," Michael Dance said.

Walt scowled at him. "What are you doing with my Harley?"

"When we showed up at Metwater's camp, looking for you, I spotted it tucked behind one of the shacks," Michael said. "I decided I'd better take it in for safekeeping before it disappeared altogether."

"Don't let him fool you," Marco said. "He just wanted to ride it."

"It's a sweet ride," Michael said, grinning.

"Metwater didn't try to stop you?" Walt asked.

"He told us you had just left it there when you decided to take off," Marco said. "That's when we knew he was lying about what happened to you. You wouldn't abandon the Harley."

"What about Lucia Raton?" Hannah asked. "Have you found her?"

"Not yet," Carmen said. "But we found a witness who saw her after she supposedly left Metwater's camp, so that seems to let him off the hook."

"For now," Graham said. "As for the rest, the assault charges are going to be tough to make stick, especially with Metwater making a stink about Kiram's death. And the kidnapping—" He looked at Hannah.

"He held me against my will," Hannah said. "But we'll probably have a hard time finding anyone except Walt who will testify to that."

"We'll see what we can do." Graham touched Walt's arm. "As of now, you're on medical leave. Get your back seen to, then go away somewhere and try to relax. Avoid the press."

"But I don't—" he started to protest, but Hannah took his other arm and he fell silent.

"Why don't you come to Texas?" she asked. "I could use some help settling in with Joy."

She didn't blame him for the doubt in his eyes. After all, she had wasted a lot of time protesting that things would never work out between them. But those moments in the fire, when they had been so close to death and he had been willing to risk everything to save her and Joy, had made her see how foolish her fears had been.

Aware of the others watching, she leaned closer to him and lowered her voice. "Please? I've decided I was right that first day I came in here—you really are the one I want to help me."

Her cheeks burned as he kissed her on the lips. His coworkers broke into applause and she pulled away, laughing. "Is that a yes?"

"It's a yes," he said. "Play your cards right and I might even stick around longer than two weeks."

"I always was a good card player," she said, a thrill running through her. She'd never been a big gambler, but right now she was willing to risk a lot to be with the man she loved.

Epilogue

Carmen Redhorse looked up from her computer terminal and smiled at the little family that had just walked into Ranger headquarters. Out of uniform and toting a baby carrier, Walt Riley was the picture of a suburban dad. The woman beside him, Hannah, had lost the pinched look that had haunted her before and now glowed with the happiness of a woman in love.

"I just stopped by to clean out my locker and my desk," Walt said, setting the carrier on a chair by the door.

"How's the back?" Carmen asked. She came over to admire the infant, who babbled and flailed her arms, chubby cheeks framing an adorable baby smile.

"It's fine," he said.

"He's got some scars," Hannah said. "But I think he's almost proud of them."

"Good for his macho cred," Carmen said.

"Where is everybody?" Walt asked.

"Marco and Ethan are at training, Michael and Lance are trying to track down a guy who's been stealing rare plants from the park, Simon is in court, the commander and Randall are at a meeting in Montrose, and I'm holding down the fort here."

"What's the latest on Metwater?" Walt asked.

"Not good," Carmen said. "The DA says we don't have enough evidence to prosecute him for anything. Lucia Raton is still missing, so the fact that her locket was found sort of near his compound doesn't mean much. Anything we have any proof for, like the assault on you, Metwater blames on Kiram, whom he says was acting without his authority or knowledge."

"Right." Walt looked like he wanted to punch someone.

"At least we proved he isn't Joy's father," Hannah said. "He has no claim on her."

"He probably contributed to your sister's death, though we'll never prove it," Walt said.

"Let it go," Hannah said. "I am."

"We're still watching him," Carmen said. "He's going to make a wrong move one day and when he does, we'll catch him."

Walt nodded. "You're right." He looked at Hannah. "And so are you. I'm going to move on."

"So you're really abandoning us for Texas," Carmen said.

"The Dallas County Sheriff's Department has an opening, so I'm going to give it a try."

Carmen turned to Hannah. "Are you sure you're ready for life with a Harley-riding cop?"

Hannah shook her head. "No more Harley," she said. "He sold it."

Carmen put a hand to her chest in a pantomime of shock. "You sold the Harley?"

Walt's cheeks reddened. "Yeah, well, you can't strap a car seat on the back of a motorcycle."

"This must be serious," Carmen said.

Hannah slipped her arm through Walt's, smiling at him with the indulgent look women in love shared. "Yes, it is."

Carmen caught the flash of the diamond on the third finger of Hannah's left hand. "How did I miss this?" She grabbed the hand for a closer look. "Nicely done, Agent Riley," she said. "Have you set a date?"

"We're thinking in the spring." He grinned.

"Congratulations," Carmen said. "You almost make me believe in true love."

"Hey, I was a skeptic, too," Hannah said.

"She just had to meet someone tough enough to call her bluff," Walt said.

"Someone who showed me I could trust myself." She squeezed his hand and Carmen felt the pressure around her heart. Why was it some people found love easily and some—like Hannah and Walt—had to fight for it?

The answer didn't really matter, she decided. In the end the prize was all that mattered, not how you came to win it.

* * * * *

COMING NEXT MONTH FROM

HARLEQUIN®

INTRIGUE

Available July 18, 2017

#1725 DARK HORSE

Whitehorse, Montana: The McGraw Kidnapping

by B.J. Daniels

The case of the infant McGraw twins' kidnapping has been a mystery for twenty-five years, and true-crime writer Nikki St. James means to crack it wide open—but the protective Cull McGraw is wary of her intentions toward his family...and toward him.

#1726 CORNERED IN CONARD COUNTY

Conard County: The Next Generation • by Rachel Lee

With a killer hot on her heels, Dory Lake seeks refuge in Conard County and protection from one of Cadell Marcus's expertly trained guard dogs—but she didn't count on Cadell as part of the deal.

#1727 PROTECTION DETAIL

The Precinct: Bachelors in Blue • by Julie Miller

Jane Boyle's life depends on her ability to keep secrets, and detective Thomas Watson doesn't realize the nurse caring for his ailing father is in witness protection...or that the sparks flying between them put them both at risk.

#1728 MANHUNT ON MYSTIC MESA

The Ranger Brigade: Family Secrets • by Cindi Myers

Ranger Ryan Spencer always follows the rules...until a murder investigation leads him to bending a few for the sake of Jana Lassiter, and breaking them completely when she's captured by the killer.

#1729 SECRET AGENT SURRENDER

The Lawmen: Bullets and Brawn • by Elizabeth Heiter

DEA agent Marcos Costa is undercover and ready to bring down a drug kingpin inside his own mansion—until he runs into Brenna Hartwell, his very first love. He doesn't know she's a rookie detective on a case, and their sweet reunion will be short-lived if their cover is blown.

#1730 STONE COLD UNDERCOVER AGENT

by Nicole Helm

Undercover FBI agent Jaime Alessandro has seen nothing but darkness as he's climbed the ranks of a crime ring. But when "The Stallion" makes him a gift of Gabriella Torres, who has been a captive for eight years, he sees her as much more than the key to bringing down the ring once and for all...

YOU CAN FIND MORE INFORMATION ON UPCOMING HARLEQUIN® TITLES, FREE EXCERPTS AND MORE AT WWW.HARLEQUIN.COM.

The kidnapping of the McGraw twins devastated this ranching family. Twenty-five years later, when a true-crime writer investigates, will the family be able to endure the truth?

Read on for a sneak preview of
DARK HORSE,
the first book in a new series from
New York Times *bestselling author B.J. Daniels,*
WHITEHORSE, MONTANA: THE McGRAW KIDNAPPING

"I want to ask you about your babies," Nikki said. "Oakley and Jesse Rose?" Was it her imagination or did the woman clutch the dolls even harder to her thin chest?

"What happened the night they disappeared?" Did Nikki really expect an answer? She could hope, couldn't she? Mostly, she needed to hear the sound of her voice in this claustrophobic room. The rocking had a hypnotic effect, like being pulled down a rabbit hole.

"Everyone outside this room believes you had something to do with it. You and Nate Corwin." No response, no reaction to the name. "Was he your lover?"

She moved closer, catching the decaying scent that rose from the rocking chair as if the woman was already dead. "I don't believe it's true. But I think you might know who kidnapped your babies," she whispered.

The speculation at the time was that the kidnapping had been an inside job. Marianne had been suffering from postpartum depression. The nanny had said that Mrs. McGraw was having trouble bonding with the babies and that she'd been afraid to leave Marianne alone with them.

HIEXP0717

And, of course, there'd been Marianne's secret lover—the man everyone believed had helped her kidnap her own children. He'd been implicated because of a shovel found in the stables with his bloody fingerprints on it—along with fresh soil—even though no fresh graves had been found.

"Was Nate Corwin involved, Marianne?" The court had decided that Marianne McGraw couldn't have acted alone. To get both babies out the second-story window, she would have needed an accomplice.

"Did my father help you?"

There was no sign that the woman even heard her, let alone recognized her alleged lover's name. And if the woman had answered, Nikki knew she would have jumped out of her skin.

She checked to make sure Tess wasn't watching as she snapped a photo of the woman in the rocker. The flash lit the room for an instant and made a snap sound. As she started to take another, she thought she heard a low growling sound coming from the rocker.

She hurriedly took another photo, though hesitantly, as the growling sound seemed to grow louder. Her eye on the viewfinder, she was still focused on the woman in the rocker when Marianne McGraw seemed to rock forward as if lurching from her chair.

A shriek escaped her before she could pull down the camera. She had closed her eyes and thrown herself back, slamming into the wall. Pain raced up one shoulder. She stifled a scream as she waited for the feel of the woman's clawlike fingers on her throat.

But Marianne McGraw hadn't moved. It had only been a trick of the light. And yet, Nikki noticed something different about the woman.

Marianne was smiling.

Don't miss
DARK HORSE by B.J. Daniels,
available August 2017 wherever
Harlequin® Intrigue books and ebooks are sold.

www.Harlequin.com

HIEXP0717